RABBIT BACK AND [...]

It was one of those mellow autumn evenings when everything was swimming in golden light. Banks of pink-stained clouds made the western sky fabulous and in the east deep purple mist was edging upwards. Tony wandered in a blissful haze. He felt drunk — drunk on the light and the warmth and the brightness of everything. *'Is she pretty?' 'Yes . . . yes . . . I suppose she is . . . in a way . . .'* Her face was round as a moon — her nose was too small — her mouth was far too big — her eyebrows were too thick. *'Is she pretty?'* Tony began to laugh. 'Yes,' he whispered. There was no one else in the street. 'Yes!' he said aloud. He started running, full of a sudden wild energy. 'Yes! Yes! Yes!' he shouted. He stuck out an arm and swung himself to a halt around a lamppost, laughing and breathless.

'She's beautiful!' he yelled into the air. 'Beautiful!'

Also by the same author
and available from Hodder and
Stoughton:

THE MOLE AND BEVERLEY MILLER
THE COST OF GOING FREE

Rabbit Back and Doubled

Allan Frewin Jones

Hodder & Stoughton

LONDON SYDNEY AUCKLAND TORONTO

First published in Great Britain in 1989 by Hodder & Stoughton Children's Books

Published in paperback in 1990 by Hodder and Stoughton Children's Books

British Library C.I.P.

Jones, Allan Frewin, 1954–
Rabbit back and doubled.
I. Title
823'.914[F]
ISBN 0-340-53237-8

Printed and bound in Great Britain for Hodder and Stoughton Children's Books, a division of Hodder and Stoughton Ltd., Mill Road, Dunton Green, Sevenoaks, Kent TN13 2YA. (Editorial Office: 47 Bedford Square, London WC1B 3DP) by Clays Ltd, St Ives plc.

Chapter 1

'Sshhh! We'll scare them!'

Tony came to a halt and stared at Chris through the tangle of leaves and branches.

'This is ridiculous,' he hissed. 'I'm going back.'

Mog, head down, ploughing through the foliage like a small bull, crashed into Tony's back and sat down unexpectedly in a sizzle of nettles. He sprang up with a shriek, clutching the seat of his jeans.

'Quiet, you berk,' growled Chris, pawing the air.

'I'm stung,' said Mog. 'What did you stop for, you cretin?' This aimed at Tony.

''Cos I'm sick of this,' said Tony, straightening up. 'There are loads of birds in the park. What on earth are we creeping about behind people's gardens for? We can't possibly get close enough to any to photograph them like this. Any bird worth a worm would hear us and be off before I even got the camera out of its case.'

'Why don't we all sing "Here we go, here we go", why don't we?' hissed Chris. 'Let 'em all know we're here.'

'Look – I'm going back – I'm cut to bits. Look at this.' He held up a wrist thinly traced with red.

They were in a narrow alleyway thickly clogged with

greenery; lithe tree limbs, straggling rose branches, nettles, weeds, and a solid blanket of convolvulus over all. On one side a high brick wall reared and on the other garden fencing hemmed them in; and in the three or four foot gap between, Chris, Tony and Mog like three flies in a green web, hot, sticky and, on Tony's part particularly, not at all amused.

Chris and Mog had turned up on Tony's doorstep; Chris with his flashy new hairstyle and his trendy clothes, Mog ginger-haired and scruffy – wearing old denims that he might as well have been riveted into. Chris went around with Mog because he thought that the shorter boy's dishevelled appearance threw his own stylishness into even sharper relief – so that the girls would faint on sight. Mog, on the other hand, used Chris as a straight man – bouncing jokes off him – sharpening his wits on Chris's dull brain and greatly enjoying himself at Chris's expense.

It was the perfect friendship: neither of them was aware of how the other was making use of him.

Tony was actually sharper than either of them and had sussed out their relationship some time ago, but it suited him to spend time with them, even though he was generally happier to be on his own. As far as they were concerned, he was a necessary audience; to Tony they were an entertainment that cost him nothing except a bit of time.

The reason for their visit, as Chris had explained it, was that his sister Penny had been given a project to do over the summer holidays that involved studying local wildlife. Tony had a new camera. Penny wanted photographs. She had left it very late and needed the photos quickly now. Chris had promised Penny that Tony would oblige. The coat-hanger grin on Mog's face while Chris was explaining all this had given Tony ample reason to suspect that there was more to the affair than met the eye. Still, he hadn't been doing anything else . . .

He had become even more suspicious when, instead of heading for a local park as he expected, Chris had very determinedly steered them to this particular place.

'Magpies,' he had said, making them sound like gold dust. 'Penny wants pictures of magpies and she said she's sure there are a pair here somewhere. She's seen them.'

'There are magpies all over the place,' Tony had pointed out.

'Not like *these*.'

And so they had dived into the undergrowth.

But Tony had had enough.

Mog was pulling at the back of his jeans. 'My arse!' he moaned. 'It feels like it's on fire. Anyone got any calamine lotion they feel like rubbing in for me?'

'Look,' said Chris, trying to sound reasonable even though a broken stump was jutting uncomfortably into his back, 'we're almost there now. It's only another couple of gardens along. We can't go back now.'

'What are you talking about?' said Tony. 'What's only a couple of gardens along?'

'The tree they live in,' said Mog, grinning again. 'You can't miss it – it's got a little sign: Mr and Mrs Magpie . . .'

'Shut up, Mog . . .' said Chris.

'Right. That does it. I don't know what you two idiots are up to but you can do it without me.'

'Oh, come on . . .'

'Sod you,' said Tony.

'Please, Tony, don't be a rat.'

'What's going on, then?'

Mog giggled but quickly stopped when Chris glared at him.

'Give me the camera, then,' said Chris. 'If you're going back at least give me the camera.'

'You'll be lucky,' said Tony, clutching his camera tightly.

Chris frowned in exasperation. 'It'll be *worth* it,' he said ardently. 'Honestly.'

'You'd better tell him . . .' said Mog.

'It's Annabel Clews . . .' said Chris.

'What about her?'

'She sunbathes topless in her back garden,' said Mog. 'Topless . . .'

Tony closed his eyes as he fell in with what was going on. He opened them to see Chris grinning sheepishly at him. 'How old are you?' asked Tony.

'Old enough to want some photos of The Clews without her bikini top on . . .' said Mog.

'And that's why I'm here, is it? So you can get me to take some photos of The Clews in her knickers, you infant? Isn't that great heap of dirty magazines you've got under your bed good enough for you?'

'It's not like the real thing,' said Chris. 'Come on, Tony, don't rat on us now – just think of it: Annabel Clews . . . just *think* about it.'

'I am thinking about it,' said Tony. 'I'm not doing it.'

Chris looked suspiciously at him. 'Don't you like girls?'

Tony felt suddenly defensive. His first thought was: yes, but I don't like the idea of creeping round taking dubious photographs of them . . . but he could feel the pressure of their eyes on him.

'After all,' said Mog, 'it's no more than you get in news-papers ever day . . .'

'And she's got one hell of a body . . .' added Chris, '. . . if she's topless she can't particularly *mind* if she's seen, can she? All those windows. And nobody would bat an eyelid if she was on the beach like it . . .'

'They might at Clacton . . .' said Mog.

'A foreign beach – Spain – you know.' Chris looked slyly at Tony. 'Or do you think breasts are obscene?' Chris chose the word 'breasts' very carefully.

'No. Of course not.'

'Well then?'

The more Tony argued against it, the more he felt the other two edging him into a corner. The unspoken thread running through their persuasive digs at him was that any normal boy would do it . . . any *normal* boy would jump at the chance.

He caved in. 'You and your rampant libido . . .' he said, trying to make a joke of the whole thing.

'Isn't that where people go swimming?' asked Mog.

'I hope it makes you go blind,' said Tony. 'I really do.'

'Wait until you see her,' said Chris. 'Just wait 'til you see her.'

'Oh, come on then. Let's get it over with.'

Chris grinned and clambered onwards.

It's not that bad, I suppose, thought Tony uncertainly, it's not like we're bursting in on her while she's on the loo or anything. And I know that sort of thing's been done before.

A springy branch slapped Tony in the face and he dragged it down. It sprang up and hit Mog under the chin.

'Oi! Watch it!'

The camera was slung on a strap round Tony's neck. Whenever he could he spared a hand to hold it tight against himself. It was a Praktica – with a zoom lens – a present from his parents for good passes in his exams.

Chris stretched upwards, trying to see over the bushes. He held a thumb up to the others. 'This is it!' he said, grinning like an open piano. 'This is it.' Beyond the sturdy wooden fence a mass of bushes rose seven feet into the air. The three boys stood crammed together.

'Well?' said Tony. 'What now?'

'Can you see anything?' asked Mog, a good six inches shorter than the other two.

'Can you?' asked Chris. Tony, the tallest, craned.

'Just bushes,' he said. 'Loads of bushes.'

'Can't you see through?'

Tony found a purchase for one foot and hoisted himself higher. 'That's better,' he said. There was something bird-like about him as he stretched to see beyond or through the bushes – something of the heron or the stork. It took him a few moments to adjust his eyes to ignore the bank of leaves so that they went out of focus and revealed the garden beyond.

'Well?' Chris was impatient.

'Yes.'

'Yes what? Is she there?'

'Hang on.' Tony brought a knee up and, by grabbing a large, safe-looking branch, lifted himself on to the top of the fence. It wobbled. He adjusted his balance.

It was a large semi-detached house at the end of a long, smooth lawn. French windows were open on to a veranda and broad white steps led down to the grass. Near the steps was a round table out of which sprouted a huge, coloured umbrella. There were some chairs and two sun-loungers. One was empty; in the other a figure was curled over apparently doing something with its toes.

'Well?'

'You prat,' was Tony's only reply.

The entire garden was awash with sunlight.

'Isn't she there?' Chris couldn't find a way up on to the fence and he was jumping up and down impatiently.

'It's not her. There's someone – but it isn't her.'

'Who then?'

'Hold on.' It was no easy task to get his camera out of its case and screw on the zoom lens without falling off his precarious perch, especially with Chris tugging at his trouser-leg and hissing like a snake.

Eventually Tony had it set and, leaning against a thick bough, he held the camera to his eye and focused the zoom.

'Oh, steaming hell!'

'Wha-at?' Chris screamed quietly.

'It's Spag Bol. You've dragged me all this way to look at Spag Bol in a bikini, you raving maniac.'

'Oh, my God,' said Mog, covering his eyes, although he was far too low to see anything. He laughed. ''Orrible! It's 'orrible. What a *sight*!'

'What's that fat cow doing there?' said Chris.

'Painting her toenails,' said Tony.

'Where's The Clews?'

'God knows.'

'He hasn't a clue,' said Mog. 'You and your lurid imagination, Harriet. The Clews sunbathing topless! Huh!' He laughed again. 'They came in search of mermaids,' he said, 'but all they found were whales.' He began to sing: 'Whale meat again, don't know where, don't know when . . .'

With a frantic effort Chris managed to pull himself up on to the fence, clinging on to Tony for support. 'Let me see,' he said. Tony handed the camera over.

Chris looked. Curled over as she was, it would have taken an exceptionally slim and elegant body to look attractive.

'God,' said Chris, 'that's repulsive. How do you take pictures with this thing?'

'You'll bust the lens,' said Mog from below.

'What do you want a picture of her for?' asked Tony.

'You're kidding? I'm not missing a chance like this. Spag Bol in a bikini? It's a riot.'

'It's the button on top – on the right. Let go, give it here, you'll break it. I'll do it.'

The feeling that they were being cruel almost made him stop, but he didn't want another long argument. Best just get it over with.

Tony clicked the button. 'Gotcha!' said Chris with a wicked laugh.

'Look! What's that?'

'Gimme,' said Chris, pulling the camera out of Tony's hands.

He panned over to the stairs. He let out a low moan. 'It's her, oh wow, look!'

Annabel Clews was awesomely beautiful – fabulously beautiful – unattainably beautiful. Chris slid the telescoped circle of the zoom lens lingeringly up her body. Long, tanned legs, the briefest of white bikini briefs, a flat golden stomach. He made incoherent, longing noises in his throat.

There was an ominous crack from beneath them. Tony grabbed at a branch as he felt his balance going. The entire tree seemed to wave hello as if to let the two girls know they were there.

Mog jumped back. There was a long creak and a rush of branches and leaves as Chris and Tony found themselves crashing backwards off the overburdened fence and down into the spiky, painful alleyway.

They heard a high-pitched voice shout something from the garden.

'Quick,' hissed Mog, already in flight. 'Skedaddle!'

It was no longer a case of not being heard — but rather a manic rush not to be seen as the three of them hurtled through the undergrowth away from the wildly sagging fence and the scene of their disastrous attempt at photographing Annabel Clews who, as myth had it, sunbathed topless in her back garden.

Chapter 2

'There's someone there,' said Annabel. She rested the tray, with its jug of lemonade and two glasses, on the table. The white sun was in her eyes but in the still heat of the afternoon one tall bush with aspirations to treehood was dancing as though in a strong breeze. 'Or is there?' She shaded her eyes with one hand.

Rachel looked up, still curled in an ungainly ball in the middle of the sun-lounger, and squinted. The end of the garden was a green blur and she had left her glasses at home. She only ever carried them about when she knew she would have to look at something particular – like a film or television – a small piece of vanity, but at least it was an aspect of her appearance she could have some control over.

'I can't see anything,' she said.

'Of course you can't,' said Annabel, walking down the lawn. 'There could be a herd of rhino cavorting in the bushes before you'd notice. Perhaps there's a cat?'

She patrolled the end of the garden, but by then the tree had become still and the boys were gone. 'Kitty? Kitty-kitty?' She came back. 'The fence is down,' she said, 'as if someone was climbing on it '

Rachel frowned. 'Who?'

'Who?' said Annabel. 'How should I know? Lemonade?'

'Please.'

They stretched out on the loungers. *'C'est la vie!'* said Annabel with a sigh.

'You mean: "this is the life",' said Rachel, 'not "that's life".'

'Who cares?' She sipped lemonade. 'I could get used to this, you know, I could really get accustomed to this.'

'Make the most of it,' said Rachel, putting her sunglasses back on. 'Term starts next Tuesday.'

'Oh, shut up, miseryguts You'll be telling me how long it is to Christmas next.'

'Um . . .' Rachel counted on her fingers, '. . . three months and . . . and twenty-one days.'

'Who cares?'

'Santa Claus . . .' said Rachel, '. . . the reindeer . . . toy shops . . . the Queen. It's her only chance to . . .'

'Rachel?'

'What?'

'Dry up, there's a love.'

Minutes swooned by. They passed quickly for Annabel in a warm haze, but Rachel quickly became bored. She was going through her D. H. Lawrence phase and had just finished *Sons and Lovers* and didn't have anything else to read. She didn't even particularly like the sun – her skin, so pale that it was almost white, just went red and flaky – and she only stayed out in it to please Annabel, who hated sunbathing alone even though she dozed most of the time and was about as much of a companion as a slowly-cooking sausage.

'Annabel?'

'What?' Sleepily.

'I'm beginning to feel all prickly and horrible . . . I think I'll put my skirt back on . . . what do you think? I don't want to get burnt.'

'You won't . . . get . . . burnt . . .' murmured Annabel. 'Don't be such a drip.'

'I can *feel* myself burning already.'

'Get into the shade, then.'

'There isn't any shade. I'll go and get my skirt. Do you want anything from inside?'

Annabel shook her head slowly.

Rachel heaved herself out of the lounger. She looked angrily at Annabel's lean, tanned body.

'I completely hate you,' she said.

'You could get me some more sun-oil. It's in the bathroom cabinet.'

Rachel padded indoors. The cool of the house was an immediate relief. She walked upstairs to get her things from Annabel's bedroom. A door slammed and there was a clatter of feet. Cornell, Annabel's older brother, swung into view round the banister.

'Hello, Tubs, you look like a lobster,' he said, as he rushed past her down the stairs and out through the front door before she could think of a reply. He was tall and golden and as beautiful as his sister. Beautiful and cruel like a tiger; leaving her bleeding on the stairs from the casual rake of his claws.

As if she didn't already know. The bikini had been Annabel's idea: 'Get some sun to your body . . . people will think you've spent the summer under a rock . . . you can't wear that horrible old swimsuit thing . . .' 'All right, all right, I'll buy it. Okay? I'll buy it. Satisfied?' Rachel closed Annabel's bedroom door behind herself. There was no one else in the house but she felt less beleaguered with a closed door between her and the rest of the world. The room was full of mirrors and a mixture of warm perfume smells. 'A boudoir,' said Rachel to herself. 'It's not a bedroom, it's a boudoir.' She tried the word over to herself, 'boo . . . dwahh.' It conjured up romantic evenings of golden-eyed men singing love songs from the garden. She caught sight of herself in a full-length mirror and cringed.

Her skirt and smock-top were on the bed. She fought her

way into them and sat on the end of the bed. She looked down at her feet. On her little toenails the bright red paint looked ridiculous. She gazed aimlessly around, feeling secure again inside a barrier of clothing.

Apart from school things, the only books in the room were obviously relics of Annabel's childhood. Rachel chose one at random, *The Children's Shakespeare*. She lay on the bed and read the simple book without interest.

'What are you doing?'

'Reading.'

Annabel stared at her. 'Indoors?'

'It was too hot.'

'You're mad.'

'I expect so.'

'I thought you were bringing me some oil . . .'

'I forgot. Sorry.'

Annabel looked at herself in the mirror. She flicked a lock of hair from her forehead and was perfect again.

'You coming out?'

'I don't think so.'

'You'll get pasty and horrible.'

'I am pasty and horrible.'

Annabel approached the bed. 'Why do you do it?'

'Why do I do what?'

'You *know*!'

Rachel shrugged.

'Come on out,' said Annabel. 'It's cooler now. There's a bit of a breeze. You'll like it.'

'Why does it matter?'

'It's no fun sprawling out there on my own. It's boring. And it doesn't help knowing Joe's sunning himself somewhere in the south of France . . .'

Joe was Annabel's mysterious boyfriend. He lived in Cambridge. She had met him through Cornell. None of her school friends had ever seen him, and she would never talk about him to them, except to say he was wonderful.

'You were asleep.'

'No, I wasn't.'

Rachel made a non-committal noise.

'Come on . . .'

'Can't you just leave me here? I'm much happier indoors.'

'No,' said Annabel, grabbing Rachel's arm. 'No. No. No. Come *on*. I'm not letting you do this.' Rachel allowed herself to be pulled up off the bed.

'Bully,' she said.

'Wimp,' said Annabel. 'Are you taking your things off?'

'No.'

'Why not?'

'I don't want to.'

'No one will see.'

They stared defiantly at one another. Rachel looked away first. No one could look into Annabel's eyes for long without going weak at the knees or breaking contact.

'Your brother's just gone out.'

'Has he? I didn't even know he was about. Anyway, don't worry about him – if he comes back he won't come into the garden . . .'

'He called me "tubs".'

Annabel laughed.

Rachel glared at her.

'I think that's sweet,' said Annabel. '"Tubs" . . . that's quite cute. It's not like being called fatty or anything. It's quite . . . cuddly-sounding. Nice. Tubs.' Annabel opened the door. 'Come on then, tubs, if you're coming . . .'

'Don't!'

'Tubs, tubs, tubs,' said Annabel, 'tubs, tubs, tubs, tubs, tubs . . .'

'I'll hit you.'

'That's better,' said Annabel. 'Do you want some ice-cream? I think there's still some in the freezer, unless we've wolfed it already.'

19

'I'm keeping my clothes on,' Rachel shouted down the stairs after her.

'No one will love you if you're all sickly-white,' Annabel called back.

'No one will love me either way,' said Rachel, following.

Chapter 3

'Well, that was a brilliant idea,' said Mog. 'Got any more where that came from?'

'It would've been all right if scrag-bag here hadn't fallen off the fence,' said Chris. They were sitting on a low wall in the estate. The pre-school infants' and mothers' one o'clock club was in full flight across a stretch of brownish grass.

'Little children . . .' said Tony wistfully, watching them playing, '. . . why does it have to happen?'

'Why what?' asked Chris.

'Puberty . . .' said Tony darkly.

'You'll find out when you get there,' said Mog, swinging his legs.

'Ha bloody ha. Look, though,' he waved his arm at the teeming hoards. 'Poor little sods. If only they knew . . .'

'What shall we do?' asked Chris to no one in particular. 'Where can we go where we can take photos of girls with no clothes on?'

'Oh, no you don't,' said Tony, holding his camera in his lap. 'I've had enough of that. I went along with you that once, but I'm not doing it again. I felt like some seedy little first-former . . . and I'm still not sure you haven't broken it.'

'It's all right,' said Chris, '. . . you're such an old woman.'

'I've only had it a fortnight. My dad'll go spare . . .'

'I don't know what you're going on about. It was only second hand . . .'

'Only? Only, you tosser? Do you know how much these things cost *only* second hand?'

'It's not broken,' said Chris tiredly. 'Don't make such a soap opera out of it.'

'Prat.'

'Prat you!'

'Children!' said Mog. 'Children!'

'What shall we do?' said Chris again. 'I'm sick of looking at these horrible little buggers. Let's go to my place and listen to some tapes.'

They slid from the wall and wandered off into the estate.

'Perhaps you could get your sister to pose topless for you?' Mog suggested to Chris.

'Don't even think about it,' said Tony.

They climbed the stairs to the level where Chris lived.

'I wonder if nudism is the answer?' said Tony.

'What was the question?' asked Mog.

'I was wondering whether this obsession with *bodies* might go away if we all wandered around naked.'

'It would if Spag Bol did . . .' said Mog.

'Oh, leave her alone . . .' said Tony, more angry with himself than he was with the other two.

'Gladly,' said Mog as they waited for Chris to find his door key. 'There isn't a barge pole long enough that I would touch her with . . .'

Tony almost felt like walking off and leaving them both to it. 'Actually,' he said, as they trooped into the narrow hall, 'I think she's okay . . .'

They stared at him. Chris screwed a finger into the side of his head.

'Batty,' said Mog.

'She's got strange eyes . . .' said Tony. 'Haven't you ever noticed?'

'She's strange all over,' said Chris.

'I don't mean strange-peculiar, I mean strange-interesting . . . like . . . oh, never mind . . . forget I mentioned it . . .'

Penny was in the kitchen. 'What are you lot up to?'

'Mind your own business,' said Chris.

'Fancy posing for some photos?' asked Mog.

'Get stuffed,' said Penny.

They piled into Chris's tiny room, draped themselves over the furniture and spent the rest of the morning listening to tapes.

'Remember when we used to play doctors and nurses?' said Rachel.

'Vaguely . . .' Annabel was only half-awake again.

'It's funny . . .' said Rachel, following her own train of thought despite Annabel's indifference, '. . . funny how sort of . . . easy . . . we were about our bodies then . . . funny how innocent it all was . . . not innocent the way adults talk about "the innocence of childhood" . . . not that sort of innocent – 'cos that sort of innocence doesn't really exist, does it? I mean, children aren't innocent in the way that their parents think – are they? All that candyfloss about innocent little children . . . and all the time we were up in each other's bedrooms taking our clothes off and having a good explore.'

'Were we?'

'Don't you remember? I can remember you and me and Becky and Cornell all playing strip poker together . . . well, strip snap actually. And Cornell lost but he wouldn't take his pants off 'cos he said it was too cold. Don't you remember? We must have been nine or ten . . .'

'. . . I don't know . . . maybe . . .'

'You must remember. I can see us quite clearly if I close my eyes. You were wearing . . .'

'Rachel?'

'. . . wearing . . . what?'

'What are you rabbiting about?'

23

Rachel turned on to her side, supporting her head on her arm. 'I'm talking about how easy things were before . . .'

'Have you got gut-rot or something? There's paracetamol in the kitchen cupboard. Over the sink.'

'You're not listening.'

'I am. I am. I'm all ears – every bit of me is ears – I just don't know what you're talking about.'

'No,' said Rachel, glumly, 'you don't, do you?'

Blindly Annabel reached for the sun-oil bottle and idly smoothed some into her shoulders.

'Why don't you get some contact lenses?' she said out of nowhere.

'What for?'

'To see through.'

'I've got glasses.'

'You don't wear them, though. And then you squint all the time 'cos you can't see, which makes your face look all piggy. If you could see properly you wouldn't go around with screwy-up eyes and that'd be your first step . . .'

'I don't look piggy.'

'All right, if you say so.'

'Do I? Oh, shit, do I go around looking like a pig all the time?'

'First,' said Annabel, counting on her fingers, 'you need contact lenses . . .'

'I don't care if I do look like a pig. So what if I do?'

'. . . second, you need to learn to use make-up properly. Third you need to go on a diet, and fourth you need some flattering clothes.'

'Oh, shut up, Clews. I don't need any of those things. You're the one who needs things. First you need to mind your own business, second you need to shut up, third you need to shut up even more, and fourth . . .' she paused, thinking.

'. . . Fourth I need to shut up even more again?' Annabel finally opened her eyes and looked across at Rachel. 'You're just annoyed 'cos you know I'm right.'

'I'm going home . . .'

'Don't be so wet!'

'I'm not wet.'

'Exactly! So stop behaving as if you are.' Annabel slewed round on the lounger. 'Stick some oil on my back, I can't reach properly.'

Chapter 4

'Never, never, never will you ever – not in a million years – ever, *ever* get off with Annabel Clews. Not ever. Never,' said Mog.

'Come right out with it,' said Chris. 'Tell me if you think I've got a chance.'

'No chance,' said Mog, splaying out his arms. 'Enn. Ohh. Chance.'

'He doesn't think you've got a chance,' said Tony.

Chris was curled up on the bed, rocking back and forwards in frustration, biting at his knees.

'She hasn't got a boyfriend at the moment,' said Chris. 'I'm sure she hasn't.'

'Look,' said Mog. 'Let's be serious about this . . .'

'She was going out with sixth-formers when she was eleven,' said Tony. 'She wouldn't touch you with sterilised gloves.'

'. . . what can you offer?' asked Mog. 'I mean, what have you got that she'd be interested in? Money?'

'Not a lot.'

'A car?'

'No.'

'Roller-skates,' said Tony. 'Rusty ones.'

'Good clothes,' said Chris. 'I've got great taste in clothes. I've got a good body – a good body which is being completely wasted at the moment . . .'

'A good body?' said Mog. 'Where?'

Chris gestured to himself. 'Here!'

'Oh . . .' said Mog. 'That one. The one that fleabitten old gorilla threw out? What's good about it?'

'I'm not telling *you* . . .'

'Dream, dream, dream . . .' said Tony.

'I'd fancy me before I fancied you,' said Chris.

'What a revolting idea,' said Tony.

'If I was a *girl*,' said Chris.

'There is one person I know who thinks you're terrific,' said Mog.

'Go on? Who?'

'Look in the mirror.'

'Dickhead.' He sighed. 'I've got to go out with her. I've got to . . . it's making me ill . . .'

'That's your angle,' said Mog. 'Annabel, please go out with me or I'll scream and scream and scream 'til I make myself sick. Threaten to hold your breath until she says yes.'

'You may as well hang yourself,' said Tony. 'She won't go out with you – not to save your life she wouldn't.'

'And we didn't even get any pictures of her,' moaned Chris, 'that I could keep under my pillow and kiss every night before I went to sleep . . .'

'I think I'm going to throw up,' said Tony.

'You don't understand,' said Chris. 'Just 'cos you're not fecund like I am . . .'

'Not what?'

'Fecund,' said Chris. 'It means . . . bursting with fruitfulness . . . you know . . .'

'Bursting with it?' said Mog. 'I bet. Shall we talk about something else?'

'What else is there?'

'School next week,' said Tony. 'And we don't have to wear

27

uniforms either.'

'Smart casual clothes,' said Chris, quoting. 'I wonder what that means?'

'It means school uniform as far as I'm concerned,' said Mog. 'I haven't got any smart casual clothes. I've got jeans and tee shirt or school uniform . . .'

'Buy some . . .'

'Ha-ha.' Mog's father had been out of work for a long time.

'How is your dad?' asked Tony.

'Fine,' said Mog. 'He was tap-dancing on the draining-board when I left.'

'He was doing what?' asked Chris.

'Tap-dancing,' said Mog stonily. 'With joy. It's a joke. Get it? It's what you do when you've been out of work for five months – dance with joy. I'm being *ironic*, Christopher.'

'Why on the draining-board . . .?'

Tony wished Chris would shut up about it.

'Because it makes a nice noise.'

'I don't understand . . .'

'Got any Coke?' asked Tony, not because he particularly wanted any, but because he could see Mog was beginning to get annoyed at Chris's obtuse questions.

'Yeah, I'll get it.'

Chris left the room.

'Can you really not afford any clothes for school? You're not going to have to go in uniform, are you?' asked Tony.

'I don't know. I could ask, I suppose . . .'

'Then why don't you?'

'"Cos it makes me feel guilty asking for new clothes when there's hardly any money about . . .'

'I could lend you a bit . . .'

'If you ever say that again I'll punch your face out through the back of your head,' said Mog softly.

They sat in awkward silence until Chris came back and threw them each a can of Coke.

'Brilliant,' said Tony. 'Now half of it will spray over the floor.'

Chris opened his can and watched the foam gush out. '. . . and that's how I feel every time I look at The Clews . . .' he said. 'Like a shaken-up can of Coke. Let's drink to me getting off with her next term.'

'Right,' said Tony, standing up, 'that's it. If you're starting on about Annabel Clews again I'm off.' He picked up his camera and slung the strap over his shoulder.

As he walked down the road and his mind began to clear he suddenly found himself wondering why a girl who looked like Rachel Ronchetti should bother painting her toenails.

'Mum! I'm home!'

Faintly: 'Up here.'

Rachel ran upstairs to her mother's attic studio. It was a huge room full of singing light.

'How's it going?'

'Not bad.' She leaned back from the easel. 'What do you think?'

It was one of her mother's fantastically intricate still lifes, less than half-finished, glowing paint vying with sepia-brushed outlines.

''S good,' said Rachel. 'Fun or money?'

'Just fun. Have a good day?'

'You always ask that, and you know I've only been with Annabel.'

'That shouldn't stop it being fun. Or should it?'

Rachel shrugged. 'It was okay.'

'You caught the sun, anyway.'

'Not like she does. She'd tan under a light bulb, that one.'

Rachel's mother saw instinctively that she was feeling a bit miserable. 'Lily-white skin used to be all the rage, you know,' she said. 'In the eighteenth century all the grand houses were built with the main windows facing north so that the women's skin never saw the light of day. It was very prestigious – pale skin – not just of beauty, but classy with it. And you've got the most glorious hair in the world, haven't you?' She reached out and stroked Rachel's rusty curls with the backs of her fingers. 'Dead Pre-Raphaelite, all those tumbly locks. Just like Jane Morris.'

'Who dat?'

'Rossetti's mistress; you know that.'

'Yes. I'd forgotten her name. Mum?'

'What, sweetheart?'

'Could we afford me some contact lenses?'

'We might for your birthday, if that's what you'd like. We've been wondering what to get you. How long's that? . . . eight weeks. Can you wait that long or is it urgent?'

'Not urgent,' said Rachel, 'just an idea.'

'Good idea. At least it'd stop you . . .'

'. . . looking like a pig. I know.'

'I wasn't going to say that. Who's said you look like a pig?'

'No one. I just think I do.'

'Rubbish. Anyway, what I was going to say was that at least it'd stop you having to remember to take your glasses with you everywhere. You know what a wozzle you are for forgetting them.'

'I don't like them . . .'

'I know that.'

'I look horrible in glasses.'

'Then you shall have some contact lenses. How's that?'

'You're the bestest mum in the world,' said Rachel, flinging her arms around her mother's neck with a sudden burst of affection.

'I know. Careful, you'll get all over paint. Go and put some coffee on, there's a good girl, and I'll be down in a minute.'

Rachel ran downstairs. She had no intention whatsoever of following Annabel's four-point plan, but contact lenses did seem like a good idea, and if it made her look less piggy . . .

Chapter 5

Halfway home Tony had been seduced off his path by the waning sun sparkling like cut glass through the immense old trees that bordered the disused cemetery. It was a magical place for Tony, a rambling, wild, neglected place blazing with life in the middle of all those dreary streets. The Victorians certainly knew how to bury people. Walking among trees he would suddenly happen upon a soaring marble tomb, guarded by angels on plinths and engraved with words that thrilled through him: TITUS SAUNDERCOCK – CALLED TO GLORY AND A SEAT AT THE SAVIOUR'S TABLE FOR ETERNITY.

Tony only ever went to the cemetery on his own, usually with a sketch-pad and a pocket full of pencils and a large packet of peanuts to 'keep him going' as his mother would say. His parents viewed these outings with subdued fascination – marvelling at the pictures he would bring back, and wondering where his talent came from.

He was expected to go to art school. Sometimes this thought puzzled him – as though he was following a will-o'-the-wisp – and sometimes it shone in front of him like a guiding light. He couldn't help himself drawing – but he often wondered how he would feel about *having* to draw – whether he wanted to or not. Would that ruin everything or make everything perfect? It was so difficult to tell.

And now he had a camera. A camera instead of a pencil. Was *that* better? He took a few shots of trees against the sky. Through the viewfinder it looked like eggshell china laced with cracks. It intrigued him how easily things became abstract once you took them out of context.

He took a close-up of a tree trunk, filling the frame with knotted wrinkles. Oak trees were never young. He was reminded of his grandfather who had first introduced him to the cemetery. 'See that one, my lad – Thomas Tilling . . . the man who started the first commercial bus route. That's where you end up, Laddo, capitalist or communist, it's all the same, all the same – six feet under and only fit for the worms . . .'

Tony walked down towards the gates. There was a lot of vandalism. Graffiti. Statues with broken limbs and missing heads. Up-ended stones. DAN WOZ ERE. He remembered being told that Lord Byron used to carve his name everywhere. BYRON WOZ ERE. Byron wasn't condemned for it – so why condemn DAN? Was Byron some scruffy herbert with a penknife or was DAN a great poet? Did it matter?

Someone had shoved the orange ball from a street-crossing lamp over the head of a praying angel. Tony was offended but intrigued. It made the angel look as though it had come from outer space. Angels in space helmets. What a strange world. Tony took a photograph of it, then went home.

Martin was on the couch under his headphones – eyes closed, feet on the arm. In passing Tony automatically turned the volume on the stereo full up and Martin jumped up with a yell as though someone had whacked a few thousand volts through him.

Grandad was sunning himself in a deckchair by the steps that led down to their small, clipped garden.

'Hello.'

'Hello, there, Laddo.'

'Can I take a picture of you?' Tony held out the camera. The zoom lens was in its carrying case, strung on to the strap.

'I don't know. Can you?' Typical Grandad.

'Will you let me?' said Tony. '*May* I, I meant.'

'You may.'

Tony set up the shot.

'Aren't you going to check the light?'

'It does it automatically,' said Tony, arranging his grandfather in the middle of the square.

'No skill in that.' Click

His grandad stretched his face into a great fangy grin. Tony couldn't hold the camera still for laughing.

'What's so funny?'

'You are.'

'All me own teeth as well.'

'I should think they are. I can't imagine anyone having the nerve to give you a set like that.'

'You cheeky blighter,' he scratched at his front teeth. 'Itchy,' he said.

'Teeth don't itch.'

'Mine do. Anyway, you should be out taking pictures of pretty girlies, not ugly old monsters in grubby shirts.'

'Chris Harriet has already had me on that . . .'

'Chris – he the one with the red hair? The scatty little one?'

'No. That's Morgan – Chris is the blond one. The big one.'

'. . . with the muscles and the zoot suits?'

'Zoot suits? What's that?'

'Flash clothes. Trendy. The trendy one.'

'Yes. That's him.'

'I got treated like a pensioner this morning . . .'

Tony was used to his grandfather's tangents. 'You are a pensioner.'

'How dare you. I might be on a pension but I'm blowed if I'm a pensioner.'

'Grandad, you're seventy-three . . .'

'Only outside, Laddo, only outside. I was in this bus queue and – bloody cheek – the conductor – the conductor mark you – said, "Come along, old chap, let me help you on." Like

I was a thundering cripple or something. "Help me on," I says to him. I told him – "I'll show you, boyo, come on," I said. "Arm wrestling. Come on . . ."'

'And did he?'

'Na-ah. I shut him up, though. He was trying to get me to go downstairs but I just went upstairs.'

'That wasn't very bright.'

'I'm not through yet.'

'No point taking risks just to be stroppy.'

'I'll be as stroppy as I like. They're not putting me out to grass. And I'll tell you something else – if your dad doesn't get round to painting my ceiling I'll bloody well do it myself.'

'You'll get dizzy. You'll fall off the ladder and you'll break your neck,' said Tony, matter-of-factly.

'How about a cup of tea, Laddo, how about a nice cup of tea?'

Tony put his camera back in its case. 'If you like,' he said, 'Grandaddo.'

'Watch yourself.'

As Tony passed, his grandfather's arm whipped out and his cupped hand slapped hard on Tony's thigh. Even though he had been expecting it, Tony wasn't quick enough to dodge and, with a yell of pain, he limped into the kitchen with his thigh stinging.

'I'll put rat poison in it,' he shouted.

Grandad, chortling to himself, rubbed his hands together and stretched out his legs in the sunlight. 'Only on the outside,' he said, 'only on the outside.

Chapter 6

As usual, the first two days of term were chaotic: take one large school, pour in twelve hundred pupils, add a scattering of good, bad and indifferent teachers; mix in a timetable that it would take Einstein to unravel, and stir vigorously.

Mog was doing things with computers, Tony was on the Arts side, and Chris and his libido were retaking their exams to try and get decent grades.

'I couldn't concentrate,' he explained. 'How can you concentrate with The Clews wafting about with all that *body* going on under her clothes?'

Annabel and her body had passed all eight of her exams with flying colours and with hardly a thought, and were already wondering whether they fancied Oxford or Cambridge where Joe was. Rachel, interested only in art, although she had to take English and history as well, was nibbling carrots and celery for lunch and trying not to squint.

And it was in this manner that the new term began.

'You promised,' said Chris.
  'No I didn't.'
  'Yes you did.'
  'I didn't.'

'Did.'

'Didn't . . .'

'I love these intellectual debates,' said Tony. 'Socrates nil, Aristotle two . . .'

'He promised, didn't he? He said he'd help?' said Chris, turning to Tony who, with his feet on the table, was reading a music paper.

'I never did, you oaf,' said Mog. 'If you recall, I said you'd never have a chance with her. That's what I said.'

'What are you doing in here, Harriet?'

Chris looked round. It was Giddings — a prefect. 'Mind your own business — dickhead.'

'Sixth form only in here.'

'I am a sixth-former . . .'

'You're retaking, aren't you?'

'Do you want a gob full of fist?'

'He's all right, Giddings, leave him alone,' said Tony.

'I was told . . .'

'We'll keep him on a lead,' said Mog. 'We'll take full responsibility, okay? He's house-trained. You are house-trained, aren't you, Harriet?'

'I am not an animal, I am a human being,' said Chris. 'Which is more than can be said for you,' looking over his shoulder at the prefect. Giddings shrugged and walked off.

'Fascist!' said Chris. 'Anyway,' he returned to more important matters, 'this is the term for the Big Push, right? I'm determined — I'm going to get a date with The Clews before half-term or my name isn't Christopher Roy Harriet — which it is, so there you are.'

Mog adopted a teacherly tone: 'Mnyaah . . . if you invested half the energies . . . mnyahh . . . you expend on chasing the female pupils of this . . . mnyahh . . . educational establishment, mnyahh . . . you would not have done so miserably in your exams, young fellow-me-lad . . .'

'That's a thought,' said Chris, 'an exam in Clews-chasing. An exam in snogging . . .'

'You'd pass fantasising,' said Tony.

'All right,' Chris leaned forward, stamping both feet for attention, 'I bet the both of you a tenner each that I get a date with The Clews before half-term. Takers?'

'I'll have some of that,' said Mog. 'Money for old rope.'

'You haven't got it,' said Tony. 'Twenty quid?'

'I don't need to have it – 'cos I'll win. Anyway, I have got it. I've got fifty quid in the building society so up yours, Anderson. Up yours.'

'So polite,' said Tony, raising his paper, 'so refined. How could she resist?'

'Of course,' said Chris smugly, 'you don't know about my secret weapon . . .'

'Not the secret weapon!' said Mog, holding his hands up. 'Not the dreaded secret weapon?'

'What is it?' asked Tony. 'A paper-bag for over your head?'

'You'll be laughing on the other side of your faces when I come in on it next Monday.'

'On what?' said Tony.

'I'm getting a motorbike.'

Tony lowered his paper. 'A motorbike? As in: a motorbike?'

'As in: brrm brrm, squeal, crash, oops, broken neck?' said Mog.

'As in: hi, Annabel, fancy a ride, hold tight, here we go . . .' said Chris. 'As in: lordy, lordy, I appear to have run out of petrol out here in the middle of nowhere, how's about a snog, Annabel?'

'As in: get your hands off me, Harriet, you bum, or I'll break every bone in your body?' said Mog.

'As in: wake up, Harriet, you're dreaming again . . .' said Tony.

'You'll see.'

'Well, here she comes,' said Mog softly, 'you going to tell her?'

Annabel and Rachel walked in talking animatedly.

'. . . and they've got themselves a flat in north London. No one's actually admitting it, but Mum and Dad have got to be subsidising them, it must be costing a fortune . . .'

'So he's moved out already, has he?' asked Rachel.

'Most of his stuff,' said Annabel. 'The guitar's gone anyway, thank God. I shan't have to listen to *that* any more at least. It wouldn't be so bad if he could actually play the thing. She must be deaf or something to put up with it – never mind putting up with him . . . Joe said . . .'

'Perhaps love's deaf as well as blind . . .'

'Love? Deaf, dumb, blind and stupid . . .' She was stopped in her tracks by Chris jumping up in front of her.

'Hello,' he said.

She stared at him. 'What?'

'All sorted out, are you? Got all your lessons sorted out?'

'Yes.' She paused. 'You're in the way.'

'Oh. Yes. Right,' Chris stepped aside. 'You doing anything interesting tonight?'

'I'm going to make an effigy of you and stick pins in it.'

'I'm getting a motorbike.'

'What sort?'

'Eh?'

'What sort? What sort of motorbike are you getting?'

'I don't know.'

'BMX,' said Mog.

'Not a push-bike,' said Chris, 'a proper motorbike – off my uncle. He's getting a new one so he's letting me have his old one.'

'Bully for you,' said Annabel, pushing past.

'I'll give you a ride on it, if you like.'

'Thanks.' Annabel and Rachel wandered off to the coffee machine.

'Next Monday. After school.'

'I'll think about it,' called Annabel, feeding money into the machine. 'Right. I've thought about it. Forget it.'

'Fifteen, love,' said Mog. 'Clews to serve.'

'We'll see,' said Chris, gazing longingly at Annabel's bottom as she bent to get the coffee cup out of the machine.

'Your eyes are the only things that will ever touch that,' said Mog quietly as Chris sat down. 'Make the most of it.'

'I'm going to die,' hissed Chris, close to Mog's ear. 'Look, you can see the outline of her knickers when she does that.'

'Stop press,' murmured Tony from behind his paper. 'Annabel Clews wears knickers – official!'

The Art Block was a separate two storey building beyond the playground, brick-built and dwarfed by the concrete mass of the main school complex. The ground floor housed all the machinery and paraphernalia of the metalwork/woodwork department, but upstairs, in a single, huge room, things were different. 'They do things differently in the Art Block,' was a common phrase in the school – a sort of 'in' joke, sparked off some time ago by an offhand comment by the headmistress who neither understood nor appreciated art on any level. She was a mathematician. If anyone can be called 'different', Tony often thought, then it must be mathematicians. They were as different as if they'd come down from Saturn. Tony did not like numbers. Numbers did not like Tony. They hated each other.

Tony was late. His first A-level art class and he was late. If Chris hadn't kept burbling on about Annabel Clews he would have been on time. He ran up the stairs. Just as he had feared – Mr Treeves was sitting on a table addressing a circle of eager faces. Tony tried to close the door quietly but Mr Treeves's head snapped round.

'Anthony Anderson, as I live and breathe, how nice of you to join us . . .'

'Sorry, I'm late, sir . . .'

'As the Americans said in 1942.' Mr Treeves pointed, straight-armed, at Tony then, swivelling his wrist without moving his arm, at a seat. 'Sit, listen, and learn.'

Tony sat.

'As I was saying,' Mr Treeves spread his hands out behind him on the table-top and lifted his grey beard to the ceiling. He looked like a prophet – a paunchy, grey-maned, scruffy prophet in stained jacket and rumpled brown cords. 'There may be some amongst you who have been thinking: A-level art – what a luscious, luxurious time I'm going to have – no books – no reading – no writing – no remembering – no effort – just two years of swanning around doing Sweet Fanny Adams until I pass out into the golden sunshine of the free world of dole queues and snooker.' He brought his hands together with a bang. 'Well, you're wrong.' His eyes were grey – you couldn't help noticing them – sometimes the grey of mist and sometimes like steel. He inspired fear or devotion – nothing in between. Tony was still not sure whether he was afraid or captivated.

'They think we're all mad, you know,' said Mr Treeves, waving to indicate the rest of the school. 'But we're not, my adolescent angels, we're not mad – we're obsessed. And if we're not obsessed yet then we soon will be. I want no one in here who isn't obsessed with art. Art isn't like . . . like physics or history or any of the other old toffee you have to chew through day by day. Art . . .' he stretched his arms out as though gathering a huge bunch of flowers '. . . is everything.' He sprang off the table and began slowly to circle the room. 'You will never work harder than in this room – this room will dominate your lives for the next two years. You will be stretched – stretched and mangled, wrung out and hung up to dry before I'm through with you. You will clamour to be let in and you will cry your eyes out when you have to go. I will turn you all into artists. Now, anyone who isn't inter-ested had better leave immediately – anyone who doesn't think they can cope had better just get up and push off now before we start.' No one moved. 'Good,' he said, 'then let the circus begin.'

He strode into his office.

'Blimey . . .' said Tony under his breath. He was on the end seat. He glanced sideways to share the feeling of having been blitzed with whoever was sitting next to him.

Rachel attempted an unsuccessful half-smile then looked away. Tony groaned inwardly. Of all the people in the world, he thought to himself, I have to sit next to Spag Bol . . . He looked round. There were fifteen people altogether apart from himself, and he would have happily sat next to any of them . . . except *her*. Bloody Harriet, he thought, blaming Chris for detaining him. He had the dreadful feeling that Treeves was the sort of teacher to say: That's your seat – stick to it, which would mean sitting next to Spag Bol for two whole years. It wasn't just that she was fat and peculiar-looking and had such a weirdly deep voice, but she was so boring. She hardly ever spoke to anyone apart from The Clews whom she followed round like a sort of pet hippo. No, that wasn't fair. She wasn't as big as that. She wasn't enor-mous; it was just that her weight problem showed up so starkly against Annabel's perfection.

Tony glanced at her again. She was pointedly looking away from him. She looks as if she feels as awkward about it as me, he thought. Perhaps she thinks I'm as boring as I think she is. The idea jarred. He suddenly wanted to say something casual and friendly to her. The oddest thing was that, out of The Clews's orbit – she seemed quite nice looking. Cuddly, he thought, in a slightly puzzled way. How strange.

In the time it took Tony to think this, Treeves had re-appeared with a sheaf of papers, sheets of which he pro-ceeded to hand round.

'For our first exercise,' he said, circling the group, 'we're going to pair off and do what it says on the paper in front of you.'

Tony read: EXERCISES

1. An Artist Cannot Work In A Void.
2. Pair Off.
3. You will each speak about yourself to your partner for one minute.

4. Your partner may *not* speak to ask questions or to acknowledge anything you say.

5. Eye contact must be maintained at all times.

A hand shot up. 'Sir!'

'What?'

'Why have we got to do this?'

'Because I say so,' said Treeves. 'Because it will be good for you. You will be spending a lot of time drawing each other in the next few weeks and you cannot draw properly without some idea of what is behind the face in front of you. Think of it as psychic dissection . . . an anatomical survey of your partner's brain . . .'

'Aren't we going to get proper models, sir?'

'I'm trying to arrange something for later in the term – meanwhile you can *all* be models. Satisfied?'

'Will we have to take our clothes off, sir?'

'Certainly not in your case, Paul, my ugly urchin, we don't want to frighten the animals . . .' There was general but uneasy laughter. 'No, my friend, we will not be taking our clothes off . . . we're doing faces. Once I've seen what you're capable of, then we'll forge on . . .'

'Aren't we doing plants, sir?'

'Plants? Fear not, you'll be doing plants – but not in here – plants are for outside . . .'

There followed a general exchange of questions and answers until Treeves held up his hands for silence. 'I'm going off for a few minutes. Sort yourself into pairs and talk in the manner explained on your papers.' And he was gone.

'Looks like you and me,' said Rachel.

Tony nodded.

'Who first?' she asked.

'Don't mind.'

'Neither do I . . .'

'Do you want to?' he asked.

'I'm not bothered.'

'Toss a coin?' She nodded and he flipped a coin.

'Heads.'

'Heads it is.'

'Does that mean I choose or I go first?'

'You go first,' said Tony quickly.

'Okay,' she looked at her watch. 'One minute.' She turned, one elbow on the table, one on the back of her chair. The eye contact was the worst bit and as they stared fixedly at each other Rachel began.

'My name's Rachel Ronchetti . . .' she half-grinned, embarrassed, '. . . you knew that . . . I'm not sure what sort of things to say . . . what am I supposed to tell you?' Tony raised his eyebrows slightly. 'I live in a big old house in Marlborough Street that my mother bought out of the proceeds of an exhibition she had ten years ago . . . oh . . . yes . . . my mother's an artist . . . I mean . . . she works, lecturing at an art college . . . and she made enough money to buy the house cash, but she couldn't do it now because house prices have gone up so much since then . . . my dad works as a secretary because he says someone's got to bring in money to pay the bills regularly and my mum's money comes in wodges instead of little regular bits . . . um . . . I've got a brother called Ben and a sister called Becky . . . Ben's twenty and he only lives at home now and then . . . Mum says he's gone all peripatetic and can't settle down and he hasn't got a job except that he does things for the council sometimes. My sister is at college learning about design and fashion and she wants to be a clothes designer in the end . . . well, I suppose she would, going to . . . well . . .' She took a breath and looked at her watch. Twenty seconds to go. 'And . . . and . . . oh God, I can't think of anything else . . .'

Tony scribbled *you* on the table and an arrow pointing at her.

'Oh . . . yes . . . I like art, especially the Surrealists and Impressionists and Pre-Raphaelites, and everyone thinks I'll be going to art school when I leave here . . . and . . . I suppose . . . after that,' frantic look at watch, five seconds '. . . I'd like to be an art teacher. Done it!' She wiped the back of her hand across her forehead. 'Phew!' she smiled in relief. 'Your go.'

'I haven't got a watch.'

She unstrapped her own and handed it to him.

'Thanks.' He waited until the display showed zero seconds then began.

'My name's Tony Anderson . . .' he grinned '. . . well, you told me who you were, didn't you?' He paused, forgetting for an instant that she couldn't reply. 'Oh . . . you're not allowed to say anything, are you?' She shook her head. 'So there's no point my asking you things . . . where was I?' Rachel shrugged then pointed to the pencilled YOU on the table and then at Tony. 'Me?' he said. 'Yes . . . me . . . oh God, this is terrible . . . my mind's gone completely blank . . . I'm sixteen, I'll be seventeen in February and then eighteen the February after that . . . when I leave school I . . . I . . . I don't know what I want to do . . . really . . .' he smiled apologetically, '. . . I'm useless at this . . . I can't think of anything . . .' thirty seconds to go, '. . . my dad gave me a camera for passing my exams reasonably well and I've been taking pictures of . . .' Now his mind really did white-out as he remembered the photograph of Rachel that he had taken. '. . . pictures . . . of . . . er . . . in . . . in Nunhead Cemetery . . . of trees and . . . and . . . those old, those old tombstone things and,' he gestured, 'you know, the tall stone thingies . . .'

Rachel mouthed something.

'What?'

She shook her head. '. . .I can't lip read . . .' said Tony with a hopeless laugh, '. . . and I can't . . .' he looked at his watch: six seconds. 'Bloody hell . . . I haven't told you anything yet.' He glanced down and the minute was up.

'Obelisks,' said Rachel.

'Sorry?'

'The tall stone thingies: obelisks they're called. It's a Greek word.'

'Yes, that's right – I went blank . . .'

44

'It is hard,' said Rachel, 'I suppose that's why he got us to do it – at least it starts people talking . . .'

'Finished?' shouted Treeves, striding out of his office. 'Splendid. Now, starting with you, Anthony, I want all of you in turn to tell us what you've learned about your partner, Come on, Anthony, up on your hind legs and tell us all about the artist to your right.'

Tony stood up and repeated everything he could remember of what Rachel had told him, thinking all the time: What's she going to tell them about me, for heaven's sake – apart from the fact that I'm an idiot?

'Good . . .' said Treeves as Tony sat down. 'Fine. Rachel. Up.'

Rachel stood up. 'My partner is Tony – I don't know where he lives 'cos he didn't tell me . . .' Tony cringed, expecting the worst. 'Tony is very interested in photography,' said Rachel, 'he's got a Zenith camera and he spends a lot of his spare time photographing the old tombs in Nunhead Cemetery – he's particularly interested in monochrome photography and is exploring the use of this medium to . . . to explore texture and the effect of light and shade and the . . . inherent problems in explaining in the format of the photograph . . . what . . . I mean, how the shapes of nature differ from man-made shapes – lines and angles and so on.' Tony stared up at her. 'He particularly likes the work of the . . . the early Surrealist photographers such as Man Ray. He also likes horror movies and . . . and hopes to become a professional photographer.' She sat down.

'Good. Right. Dennis, your go.'

'How did I do?' hissed Rachel

'Shush!' said Treeves. 'No rabbiting. Dennis, carry on . . .'

Rachel, looking at Dennis, was turned away from Tony so he couldn't catch her eye – not that he had a clue what he would say if he did.

Later on in the lesson Treeves gave them a long lecture on 'looking' and then set them another exercise that was, in its own way, even more peculiar and unsettling than the one-minute talk had been.

'Take half an hour over this,' said Treeves. 'With your partners – that's a quarter of an hour each unless my maths has escaped me completely – I want you to draw an eye – just one – upside down. That's all. One upside-down eye. Paper and pencils over on the side. Get on with it.'

'Sir?'

'Too complicated for you?' He marched over and in a few seconds had arranged two boys – one lying on his back across the table and the other sitting so that he was looking down on his partner's upturned face. 'There! That – or versions of. Get on with it.'

Tony and Rachel looked blankly at each other.

'He's barmy, isn't he?' said Tony.

Rachel shrugged. 'Best humour him,' she said. 'You can do me first.'

They arranged the chairs so that Rachel leaned backwards in hers, resting her head on the table. Tony, round the other side, found it best to kneel on his chair so he was actually over Rachel as he drew.

'I get it,' he said, sketching carefully, 'it's just a follow-up to what he was saying about looking. Your eye looks completely different upside down. I mean, the lids are all different and everything. Very odd.'

'Not as daft as he sounds, perhaps . . .' said Rachel.

'Where did you get all that stuff you made up about me?'

'I had to say something.'

'What was that name you mentioned? Man something?'

'Man Ray.'

'I've never heard of him. Anyway, my camera's a Praktica, not a Zenith.'

'Sorry. I don't know much about cameras.'

'Neither do I really.' They smiled at each other. 'It was good, though.'

He drew, trying to differentiate between the blues and

greens and golds of her iris, the different ivories and creams of the 'white', and the various tones of her skin. The deeper he looked into her pupil the more he became aware that not only his own face, but a vast amount of the room was reflected in grey shades that had no real black in them at all.

'There's no end to this . . .' he murmured, bending closer, '. . . the nearer I get the more I can see reflected . . .'

'It's magic!' said Treeves. Tony looked up – he had been too absorbed to notice the coming of the teacher. 'It was there all along and you never knew.'

'It's incredible . . .' said Tony, '. . . I can see the whole room . . .'

'Your fifteen minutes are up – time to swap over.' He tapped Tony's drawing with his forefinger. 'Very good,' he said, 'I think I may be able to do something with you. Rachel? Don't think you can freewheel because of your background – I want miracles from you.'

They swapped round. Tony found it much more difficult lying passively while Rachel drew. His eyes still traced the extraordinary confusion of colours in her iris and even after half an hour he still couldn't decide whether blue or green predominated or whether the blues and the greens and the browns and golds were all just independent flecks that formed a new, unnameable colour that was completely unique to her. It was fascinating, whatever it was.

Chapter 7

'What colour are my eyes?' asked Tony.

'Sky-blue-pink,' said Martin, 'will you get out of it – I want to clean my teeth.'

'No, come on, what colour are they?' Tony leaned over the sink. Martin stared into the mirror for a couple of seconds, looking at his brother's reflection.

'Dog-poo brown,' he said. 'I want to clean my teeth.'

Tony picked up his brother's toothbrush and, almost as though in passing, dropped it down the lavatory bowl. 'Oops,' he said, 'sorry.'

Martin yelled some abuse and shouted for their mother.

Tony took the stairs in threes and was out of the house before recriminations began.

He was a few minutes late, and by the time he had negotiated the narrow roads between the estate blocks to where the lock-up garages were, Mog and Chris were already standing waiting.

'Come on,' shouted Mog, 'he won't open up 'til you get here.'

Chris pulled out a key and held it up. 'Ladies and gennle-menn-n-n,' he proclaimed, unlocking the garage door. 'Pre-e-senting . . . the one and only . . .' he turned the handle, and wrenched the door open, '. . . Christopher Roy Harriet's new motorbike. Ta-raaah!'

Tony and Mog looked into the grey shed. 'Where?' said Mog.

'There,' said Chris, pointing at the small motorbike.

'Where?'

Chris grabbed Mog's collar and marched him into the garage and up to the motorbike. 'There.'

'Oh, yes,' said Mog, 'I couldn't quite focus on it from that distance. I used to have one like that when I was a kid. Do you wind it up with a key or has it got an elastic band? Mine had a little man in a white suit sitting on it . . .'

Chris clutched his ribs. 'I'm dying laughing, Mog, look at me, I'm dying of laughter.'

'Mine was in a box, too . . .' said Mog, undaunted. 'Has yours got a box?'

Tony leaned against the garage door. The setting evening sun was blazing red between two blocks of flats, bathing the brickwork pink and the windows a deep, sandy yellow. Even the shadows, sharp and dense, had colours in them. That bloody Treeves, he was thinking . . . I can't look at anything without wondering how to draw it these days.

'It can do seventy,' said Chris.

'On one bottle of paraffin?'

'What make is it?' asked Tony, not really interested, except in the fact that the inside walls of the garage were dyed a smoky coral colour by the sunlight.

'Yamaha. Can't you read? Yamaha 125.'

'Is that good?' asked Tony.

'For a synthesiser,' said Mog, 'not for a motorbike. This Japanese stuff is all crap . . .'

'Oh, yes? What do you know about it?'

'Everyone knows that. They're just hair-dryers on wheels.'

'You have just blown your chance of a ride, Alton,' said Chris.

Mog buried his face in his hands in mock despair.

'Tony? Fancy a ride?'

'If you like. Got crash helmets?'

'Yes. Two.'

While they were strapping their helmets on Mog was leaning over the motorbike, making the sign of the cross over it. 'In nomine Patris, Filii et Spiriti Sancti . . .' he intoned.

'Shut up and get out of the road,' said Chris.

'Careful,' shouted Tony as the motorbike wobbled across the street.

'Just keep still,' said Chris, 'roll with it . . .'

'Have you got a licence?' yelled Tony as they drove out on to the main road.

'Don't worry. Just hang on.'

Tony did hang on. It was exciting and slightly frightening – frightening that someone else was at the controls and that he, Tony, had no say in whether they bombed off down the road at seventy miles an hour or swerved off bang into a tree. Not that Chris actually did seventy. Or hit a tree, for that matter.

They left the estate behind and Chris headed for the back streets. Up the hill and round and down, and then Chris took a right into Marlborough Street. I might have known, thought Tony.

Rachel lived in one of these large Victorian houses but Tony didn't know which one. More importantly, so far as Chris was concerned, Annabel Clews lived in the fifth house along at the far end. They pulled up on the opposite side of the road.

'What are you up to?' asked Tony.

'Nothing.'

'If you think I'm sitting here all night waiting for you to get a glimpse of The Clews . . .'

Chris climbed off. 'Stay here. I'll be back in a tick.'

He walked across the road, pulling something out of the inside pocket of his jacket. He ran up to the door, pushed the whatever-it-was through the letter-box and dashed back.

Mog was sitting cross-legged in the middle of the garage

floor, reading the Instruction Manual. 'You took your time,' he said.

'What was that?' asked Tony, pulling his crash helmet off.

'Just a letter.'

Mog stood up. 'What's all this?'

'What sort of letter?'

'Just a letter . . .'

'What letter?' asked Mog.

'That's what I want to know. He's stuck a letter through The Clews's front door. Come on, Harriet, out with it. What are you writing to The Clews about?'

'It's a private letter and it's got nothing to do with you,' said Chris.

'Except that you wanted to make sure you were seen posting it,' said Tony.

Chris shrugged. 'I didn't want to leave the bike.'

'Is it a love letter?' asked Mog, grinning. 'Have you written The Clews a love letter?'

'No . . .' said Chris defensively, '. . . not . . . exactly . . .'

There was a crowd round the sixth form notice board when Tony and Mog arrived at school the next morning. There was a lot of laughter and a number of variations on 'Ahh, how *sweet!*'

'What's all the excitement?' asked Mog, too short to see.

Tony leaned above the bobbing heads. A card was pinned to the board. It had flowers on the front. Some fingers held it open so the inner writing could be seen. 'Oh my Ga-ahd!' groaned Tony.

Tony reached over the heads and took the card down.

There was a general groan and someone said: 'Spoilsport.'

Mog read it. 'What a cow . . .' he breathed. Tony crammed the card in his back pocket. He looked around. Annabel Clews was nowhere to be seen. She must have come in early, pinned it up, and gone off again.

A few minutes later Chris walked in. He was greeted by

a loud derisive cheer and a round of applause.

'What's going on?'

Tony, in one of the armchairs with his feet up on the table, pulled out the card and waved it at him.

Chris snatched it out of his hand. 'It was on the board,' said Tony. 'And Annabel has got two ns.'

Chris tore the card in half and dropped it in the bin. He looked defiantly at the sea of grinning faces. 'It was worth a try,' he said loudly. 'A bloke's entitled to a try.'

Tony smiled, impressed at Chris's bravado in the face of a humiliation that would have had him crawling under the carpet in horror.

'Well done, that Harriet,' said Mog. 'You tell 'em.'

A hush went round the room. Annabel and Rachel were standing in the doorway. Annabel's eyebrows were slightly raised, but otherwise her face was expressionless.

Chris looked quite calmly at her. 'Hello,' he said, across the room. 'You got my note, then?'

'Clever boy,' said Annabel.

'Is it a date, or not?'

Annabel's eyebrows rose even higher. 'Not,' she said.

Chris shrugged, picked up a magazine and began to flick through it, cool as anything.

Rachel caught Tony's eye and tapped her watch. Tony looked up at the wall clock. Two minutes to art. He nodded, picked up his bag, and the two of them set off for the Art Block.

It was hands today.

'Forget that you know what hands are,' said Treeves. They had got used to the way he circled round them as he spoke and didn't find it as daunting as they once had. 'Forget that you have ever seen a hand before in your entire life. Think of it as some exotic object from . . . from Easter Island – some sort of living pagan artefact that has got nothing to do with holding pencils, doing buttons up or picking noses.' He

clapped his hands together. 'No . . . better . . . better – pretend it's an animal – a separate animal that you've never seen
before. Remember it's bones . . . remember it's full of blood –
remember skin is transparent. Go!'

'There's method in this madness . . .' said Rachel, outlining
the shape of her hand with bold strokes that Tony envied.

'I can never get perspective right . . .' said Tony. His drawing method was to start from a corner and let the picture
develop like something growing.

'It's easy . . .' said Rachel.

'For you.'

They worked in silence for a while.

Treeves walked past. 'You ought to work in charcoal,' he
said to Rachel. 'Pencil does nothing for your style.'

While Rachel was off gathering fresh paper and charcoal
Treeves sat on the edge of the desk, looking at Tony's work.

'You've got a long way to go,' he said. 'You know that,
don't you?'

Tony looked up. 'Miles,' he said.

Treeves floated his fingers over the work. 'The detail is
good – you're looking properly at last, but there's no . . .
there's no heart to it. Know what I mean?' He smiled. 'I mean
that – do you know what I mean?'

'I'm not sure.'

'You're capable of being a good draughtsman – I can see
that there's talent in you somewhere, but you're not getting
through to it. Are you bored?'

'No.'

'Not even a bit? Go on, admit it – does drawing hands bore
you?'

'P'raps . . .'

'Do you think Rembrandt was bored when he did Saskia's
hands?' Tony looked blankly at him. 'The picture of her in
the fancy costume – in the National Gallery. Don't you dare
tell me you haven't been to the National Gallery . . .'

'Not . . . recently, particularly.'

Treeves put his hands round Tony's neck, pretending to strangle him. 'Get to the National Gallery,' he said. 'Go this weekend. If you haven't been there by next time I see you I shall throttle you. Got it?'

Rachel came back. Treeves slid off the desk. 'Rachel – this Thing hasn't been to the National Gallery. Make sure he does. Take him yourself if you have to – but get him there.' He tapped Tony's head. 'Exercise one,' he said, to the rhythm of his hand, 'An Artist Cannot Work In A Void.'

'He's just more or less told me I'm crap . . .' said Tony after Treeves had wandered off.

Rachel couldn't think of anything to say. 'No, you're not,' just sounded like a platitude, and, 'Yes, he's right,' would not only have been cruel, but untrue as well.

'I'm fed up with this . . .' said Tony softly, lightly doodling over his drawing. Rachel made a sympathetic face, then arranging her left hand on the table, began scratching in thick, confident outlines.

Tony watched her working for a while. He glanced at her face. Her tongue-tip was just showing between her lips. He began idly to pencil her profile. But he did it all wrong, because he was drawing what he thought a profile ought to be and not what was actually happening in front of him. He looked more intently. He noticed for the first time that her lips and nose stuck out the same distance. Small nose, large lips. He carefully filled in the bevel of her mouth, smiling slightly as he drew the little pink tip of her tongue. He began to draw in the profile, taking the line of her lips to the corner, to that small upward curve that gave the impression of being about to break into a smile.

'My eyes are beginning to go,' she said. 'I'd better get my glasses.' She always waited until her head was aching before she would succumb to the hated face-furniture.

'Don't. Not for a minute . . .' said Tony. 'Don't move for a minute.'

She kept her head quite still, but she couldn't help trying to swivel her eyes to see what he was doing. Her tongue had vanished.

'I'm getting a stiff neck,' she said after five or so minutes.

'Okay. Go on, then.'

She leaned over to see what he had drawn. 'It's me,' she said.

'More or less . . .' said Tony.

'Do I stick my tongue out like that? Stupid creature.'

'It doesn't look stupid.'

'I think so.'

'It doesn't . . .'

'Oh, yes it does . . .' she said like a character in a pantomime.

'Oh, no it doesn't,' replied Tony in the same way and they both laughed.

'What's all the merriment?' asked Treeves, appearing out of nowhere. Tony tried to cover the picture up but it was too late.

Treeves pulled it to one side and leaned over it, both hands on the table-top. There was a long silence. Tony felt acutely embarrassed.

'That's it,' he said at length, tapping the paper with his knuckles. 'That's the first positive thing you've done since you've been here. That's the first thing I've seen by you that says: Anthony Anderson was here. Do some more. Rachel won't mind. She's used to being a model.'

'I shan't stick my tongue out next time,' said Rachel, '. . . it makes me look ten pence short of a pound.'

'Vanity has got nothing to do with beauty,' said Treeves, and he was off again, leaving the remark hanging unexplained in the air.

'Can I?' asked Tony. 'Would you mind?'

'What? Sitting? Do you mean sitting properly?'

'What would that involve?'

'I don't know. It depends what sort of pose you'd want.'

'On one leg – holding a vase in the air . . .'

'You'll be lucky.'

'Draped over a chaise longue wearing only a diaphanous nightie . . .?' Tony had no idea what diaphanous meant but it sounded good.

'I'll do you like that, if you like,' said Rachel, who knew exactly what diaphanous meant. 'Anyway, my nightie is a sensible cotton one with long sleeves and a high neckline. It'd be like drawing me with my head sticking out through the top of a tent.'

'Just your face, then. Just a portrait.'

'Okay. You're on. How, though?'

'How though, what?'

'How are you going to set it up? Mr Treeves isn't going to be very amused at me just sitting there gazing into space for a few hours while you draw me. He's not likely to see that as a very productive use of my time.'

'I could draw you drawing something else . . .'

'If that's what you want . . .'

'No,' Tony frowned thoughtfully, 'it's not . . . really. I wouldn't be able to see your eyes properly. I'd really like to do one of you looking straight at me so I can have a proper go at getting your eyes right.'

Rachel chewed her top lip thoughtfully. 'I'll tell you what,' she said. 'I'll have to ask . . . but my mum might let us use her studio. I'm sure she wouldn't mind – not if she knew we were being serious about it. She can't stand people mucking about up there but if I tell her it's proper, kosher homework – which it would be – I'm sure she'll let us. There's gorgeous light up there and it's a really good atmosphere to work in.'

Tony smiled. 'A proper studio?'

Rachel nodded. 'A one hundred per cent, fully fledged, ultra-proper studio.'

'Wow.'

Chapter 8

'Your grandad's not very well – pop up and ask him if he wants anything.'

Tony slung his bag over a chair. 'What's wrong with him?'

His mother made a non-committal movement of her shoulders. 'Only a cold, I think . . .'

Tony ran upstairs and knocked on his grandfather's door. 'Coo-ee? Anybody home?'

'That you, Laddo?'

His grandfather was sitting up in bed in an explosion of pillows. His pale face highlighted the blue veins and deep wrinkles and the fierce, two-day stubble on his chin. Tony wished he could stop thinking of people as prospective drawings.

'How's you?'

'I'm all right. Your *mother* . . .'

'Do you want anything?'

'Yes,' his grandfather pointed upwards, 'my bloody ceiling painted . . .' Years of hand-rolled cigarettes had toned the ceiling to a blotchy sepia. 'It's been driving me mad. I've been lying here staring at it all day.'

'Tell Dad. It's no good telling me.'

'Your father? He's neither good to man nor beast. It'll be

Christmas before he gets round to it. Bloody Christmas. *Next* bloody Christmas. Next year.'

'Oh, I'll do it, for Gawd's sake . . .'

'Don't you take the Lord's name in vain, my boy. Don't you swear in front of me.'

'Me swear in front of you? That's a good one.'

'I never swear. I may use bad language on occasion, but you'll never hear blasphemy from me . . .'

'Yes, all right,' Tony looked up. 'Sorry, God – didn't mean it.'

'Struck by lightning, you'll be. Struck by a bolt of lightning, you 'orrible 'eathen.'

'Won't be able to do your ceiling, then, will I?'

'It'll need two coats. You do it properly, now. No pansified split-splatting – I want all the corners done, and none on the walls.'

'Yessir!' said Tony, saluting. 'Is there anything else His Eminence requires?'

'A cup of tea. I haven't had a cup of tea since two o'clock. Three hours ago. She'd let me die of thirst up here, she would. Die of thirst. She'll come up one day and there'll be just a load of old bones sitting up in rags of pyjamas with its tongue hanging out.'

'You don't half push it sometimes,' said Tony from the door.

His grandfather grinned, showing all his horrible brown teeth. 'I know,' he cackled. 'Good, innit?'

'Mum? Mu-um?' Rachel came crashing into the lounge wearing only a smock-top and socks.

'What? What-what-what-what-what?' Mother and elder daughter were crawling about on a floor strewn with a mess of patterns and material.

'Don't clodhop all over this,' shouted Rebecca, fending her sister off with both hands.

'There's pins everywhere,' warned her mother. 'Stand by

the door or you'll get them in your feet. I've told you about
socks. You'll slip and hurt something.'

'Never mind all that,' said Rachel. 'I've lost half a stone.
Half a stone in just two weeks.' She waited to be praised.

'Pass that arm-bit over, Mum,' said Rebecca. 'There's just
room to pin it on the end here . . .'

'Have you really, Rachel?' said Rachel. 'Half a stone?
That's very good, Rachel. You are being good, Rachel, keeping to your diet like that.'

'What do you weigh now, then?' asked Rebecca.

'. . . Less . . .' said Rachel guardedly.

'Less than what?'

'Less than eleven stone . . .' said Rachel.

'Eleven stone? You're not eleven stone, are you?'

'No. I said: *less* than eleven stone.'

Her mother sat up on her haunches. 'You carry it all right,'
she said. 'You're tall enough to carry a bit of excess without
looking gruesome.'

'I don't know that I'd go that far . . .' said Rebecca.

'You can talk . . . at least I'm trying . . .'

'Trying what?' said Rebecca.

'To lose weight. At least I'm not wallowing in it like you
are . . .'

'But, you see, I don't *care*,' said Rebecca. 'I don't overeat, I
get exercise from my yoga and from swimming; if I'm big I'm
big. What's the huge deal about it? And Steve likes me the
way I am – and he's the only other person whose opinion I
care about.'

'Well, I *do* care, I don't want to be podgy all my life . . .'

'It's puppy fat . . .' said her mother.

'At sixteen? You're joking? It's full-grown *dog* fat and I
want to shift it.'

'Carry on, then,' said Rebecca coldly. 'You'll never end up
looking like Annabel no matter how much you lose. You're
all the wrong shape.'

'Thanks for the vote of confidence.' Rachel slammed the

door behind her. She slipped on the polished wood of the landing and hit her knee on the stairs. She limped off to the kitchen and nibbled at a raw carrot. With a despairing sigh she threw it in the bin and went to the bread bin. A couple of slices of toast, she thought. That won't do any harm.

'I hope you appreciate this, you miserable old sod,' said Tony from the top of the stepladder.

'No one's making you,' said his grandfather. 'You wouldn't begrudge your grandfather a lick of paint?'

Tony stretched to dab paint into the corner. 'I'm supposed to be off in Marlborough Street doing a portrait of a pal from school.'

'Not that ugly little ginger-headed tyke, I hope.'

'No. Not Mog. A girl, actually.'

'Is she pretty?'

Tony paused. 'Yes . . .' he said slowly, '. . . yes . . . I suppose she is . . . in a way . . .'

'That's the idea. I know,' he tapped Tony's leg with his tobacco tin. 'What colour eyes?'

'Sky-blue-pink,' said Tony automatically.

'You can always tell . . .'

'Sort of greeny-blue with little gold and red and brown and yellow flecks. They go more yellowy and greeny in sunlight and more bluey in the shade. And sometimes you just can't say what colour they are . . .' Tony came out of his short reverie and looked down at his grandfather. 'You can always tell what?'

'Don't you know?'

'Don't grin at me like that – it makes you look demented.'

His grandfather began to whistle a tune Tony didn't recognise.

'What's that?'

'Ask your mum . . .'

'What is it?'

'Ask her . . .' he whistled again, a slow melody of about

seven notes, '. . . you ask her what that's called . . .'

'What are you up to?'

'Annabel! Good. I need you.' Rachel's bedroom was strewn with clothes as though she had opened her wardrobe and dragged out every drawer and simply flung everything around in a mad frenzy.

'Having a jumble sale? God, look at this.' She held up a gymslip.

'I want everything I don't wear chucked out,' said Rachel. 'I'm autumn-cleaning . . .'

'Why now? I've been on at you for years . . . why all of a sudden?'

'It's my birthday next month,' said Rachel. '. . . I always get money. I'll be able to buy new stuff.'

'Why?'

Rachel stood up, her arms full of jumpers. 'Why not?'

'Why not. But why?'

''Cos I feel like it. Part four of the four-part plan: get new togs, remember?'

'. . . and I got a right mouthful from you about that . . .'

'I changed my mind.'

'All of a sudden . . .?'

'All of a sudden.'

'And you're on a diet . . .'

'And I'm on a diet – and I'm getting contact lenses for my birthday – I've already been to the optician's and they'll be ready Tuesday week. And I'm going to have a party. Mum's already agreed . . .'

Annabel bounced on to the bed. 'You're having me on,' she said.

'How's that?'

'This is nothing to do with my four-part plan – this is nothing to do with me . . .'

Rachel's head vanished into her wardrobe.

'Is it?' said Annabel.

'I think this can go . . .' said Rachel, holding up a pair of white dungareees covered in coloured patches. 'I can't see myself wearing these any more . . .'

'You're a charlatan, Rachel Ronchetti . . .'

'I don't know what you're talking about . . .'

'Is it that Tony Thingie? It is, isn't it? It's Tony Whatsit . . . Anderson . . .'

'Rabbit, rabbit, rabbit . . .' said Rachel.

'My God . . .' Annabel stared at her, an astonished smile on her face. 'My . . . God . . .'

Rachel grabbed up an armful of old skirts and hugged them to her. 'Rabbit, rabbit . . . rabbit, rabbit, rabb . . . it!'

'"Hearts and Flowers",' said Tony's mother. 'It's called "Hearts and Flowers". It's what they used to play in the background over all those soppy old love story films. The old silent ones with Rudolph Valentino and people like that. On a violin. "Hearts and Flowers".'

'Oh.' Tony stared into his dinner plate.

'Why?'

'Nothing.'

His grandfather's eyes were gleaming. 'Better ask our laddo who, not why,' he said.

'Who?' Tony's father looked round from the television. 'Who what?'

'Who what nothing,' said Tony, blushing infuriatingly. 'He's just being funny . . .'

His grandfather began to sing in a terrible, cracked voice, 'Birds do it, bees do it, even educated fleas do it . . .'

'I'm off,' said Tony, getting up.

'Finish your dinner . . .' said his mother.

'I can't. I'm not hungry. I'm off out. See you.'

'Out where?' called his father.

'Over to Chris. I won't be late.'

'See to it.'

The warm evening air calmed him as he walked slowly

down the road. It was one of those mellow autumn evenings when everything was swimming in golden light. Banks of pink-stained clouds made the western sky fabulous and in the east deep purple mist was edging upwards. Tony wandered in a blissful haze. He felt drunk — drunk on the light and the warmth and the brightness of everything. *'Is she pretty?'* 'Yes ... yes ... I suppose she is ... in a way ...' *'Is she pretty?'* 'Yes ... yes ...' Her face was round as a moon — her nose was too small — her mouth was far too big — her eyebrows were too thick. *'Is she pretty?'* Tony began to laugh. 'Yes,' he whispered. There was no one else in the street. 'Yes!' he said aloud. He started running, full of a sudden wild energy. 'Yes! Yes! Yes!' he shouted. He stuck out an arm and swung himself to a halt around a lamppost, laughing and breathless.

'She's beautiful!' he yelled into the air. 'Beautiful!'

Chapter 9

The bedroom door came flying open. 'Rachel! What on earth are you doing?'

Rachel crashed down on to her knees on the bed. 'I'm trampolining!'

Her mother laughed, hanging on to the door as if to steady herself. 'You raving maniac.'

Rachel scrambled to her stockinged feet and bounced from foot to foot, balancing herself with outstretched arms. 'It's good for me,' she said. A foot became entangled in sheets and she sat down heavily to a plaintive creaking of wood.

'Elephant!' said her mother. 'You'll break it.'

'No I won't, look . . .' she knelt up, her thumbs pushed down the waist of her jeans. 'I haven't been able to get these on for about three years. Look. They're loose. It's actually beginning to work.'

'Good for you . . . just so long as you don't get carried away . . .'

'Oh, I won't break it – I just had to leap around a bit, that's all . . .'

'I meant the diet. Don't get carried away with the diet.'

Rachel grasped two handfuls of stomach. 'I think I've got a bit to go yet,' she said.

'You've got to eat properly. Weren't you wanting my studio this afternoon?'

'Not now. He's been shanghaied into painting his grandfather's bedroom ceiling. He's coming round tomorrow morning. That's all right, isn't it? You're not working up there tomorrow, are you?'

'What about Aunt Lucy?'

'What about her?'

'We're all supposed to be going to visit her tomorrow, wozzle-bonce. You haven't half got a convenient memory at times.'

'I've asked Tony round now. Do I have to go?'

'Can you be trusted?'

'Trusted to do what?'

'You're not just jumping around 'cos you've lost weight. I know that look of yours. The same as when you won first prize in that competition. Remember? You had to do a drawing of how a modern zoo should look – a design – and the prize was a day at London Zoo for the whole family.'

'That was . . . Mother! That was six years ago.'

'You haven't changed,' said her mother. 'Heart on your sleeve still. You'd be the world's worst poker player.'

'I can be happy, can't I?'

'Yes. Just don't be so noisy about it.'

Rachel let out a scream of joy like a locomotive letting off steam. Her mother put her hands over her ears.

'They'll think I'm murdering you – lunatic!'

'Rabbit, rabbit, rabbit!' shouted Rachel, bouncing on all fours.

'It'll be white coats and butterfly nets,' warned her mother, closing the door on her way out.

Rachel ran to the window, pressing her cheek against the cool pane and spreading her hands out as if she would just like to throw herself out into the glorious crimson sunset.

'Tony! You're late. I was just going to phone.'

'Sorry. My delightful grandfather found some bits I'd missed. In corners. He was up there with a torch looking for any little edges I'd missed.' Rachel pulled the door fully open and Tony stepped into the hall, his blue art-folder under his arm. 'I couldn't believe it. I was halfway out of the front door when he called me back. I had to get changed back into my old clothes and finish it off. I felt like dipping his head in the paint and using him as a brush.'

'All done now though?'

'Oh, I expect he'll find some more, but he'll have to whistle for it now I've escaped.'

'I've got some coffee on. Do you like Kenyan?'

'I don't know.'

They had coffee and home-made biscuits in the kitchen then Rachel took Tony up to her mother's studio.

'They're all out,' she explained. 'I'm supposed to be as well, but I forgot.'

'We can leave it, if you like . . .'

'No. They've gone now. Anyway, my Aunt Lucy is a pain. She's a vegetarian . . .'

'Oh, dear . . .'

'And a socialist, and a feminist and an ecologist. Every time I see her I come back with my ears buzzing. She runs a health food shop called Beans and Things: everything from lentils to biodegradable washing-up liquid . . .'

'I suppose it's all in a good cause . . .'

'No. Not her. It's just a pose, something to keep her mind off the fact that she married a right turkey. Daniel. Daniel the Wimp. Anyway,' she opened the studio door, 'what do you think?'

Tony had never been in a real studio before. It was under the eaves of the roof. Light poured in through a long skylight, shimmering off the white walls and shining on the paint-spattered floorboards so that the densest of shadows were only a pale, diffused grey.

An easel was shrouded in white sheeting. Canvases were

stacked against the walls and all was in a flux of creative disorder.

'Is she painting this?' asked Tony, staring down at a still-life collection on a dark-wood table-top. There was an open jewel box, a doll, a candelabra, an open bible, chess pieces, and a scattering of intricate jewellery, all of which reflected darkly in the wood.

Rachel nodded, pointing at the easel.

'It'd drive me mad,' said Tony.

'She already is.'

They pulled two chairs close together.

'You can read or something,' said Tony. 'If you want to.'

'No. I'm okay.' Tony propped his drawing-board across his knees. He stared at her face for a long time before he made any marks. He had brought five different densities of pencil, from B2 to B5 and a B12 which was very soft and as black as charcoal.

They had got used to intense eye contact and they were able to examine each other's faces with a candour that would have been impossible under any other circumstances.

'Is my hair how you want it?' said Rachel, trying not to move her lips.

'Can you take it off your forehead a bit?' Rachel pushed back a tangle of curls. 'Yes, that's better.'

With a deep breath, Tony began the drawing.

It took him over an hour to get the width of her face right – an hour, while she gazed at him and he took the curve of her cheek over and over again until, suddenly, he knew it was right.

'My great-grandfather was Italian . . .' Rachel told him in answer to a question about her surname, '. . . he came over in the late nineteenth century. He married an Irishwoman and they had about twenty kids. He was quite well-off, apparently. He owned a fleet of hansom carriages. Then some swine invented motorcars and he went bust in five years. Flat as a frog in the road. My grandfather was a sign-writer. My dad can tell you how he used to take him round London and show him all the bits of writing he'd done on shop fronts, and all the gold-leafing. It's probably all gone, now, but at least it outlived him – made him feel a bit permanent, anyway. I often wonder if anything I do will outlive me. It'd be nice wouldn't it – to think that something you created would just – sort of – carry on? Like a painting or . . . or, I don't know – a garden. A garden you'd planted out yourself so that people could walk in it and they'd be sort of walking through your imagination . . .'

Tony nodded, concentrating too intently to reply but enjoying the husky warmth of her voice.

Two hours passed. Tony hardly said a word, but Rachel would often break into some new story about her family or herself – giving things away to Tony that she had never spoken about to anyone else – things that even Annabel didn't know.

'I used to steal money out of my father's pockets when I was about twelve,' she said, 'and I would buy loads of bars of chocolate and go off on my own and stuff myself silly. I used to eat until my stomach hurt. You know – when you eat too much and your stomach is so full that you're almost sick – like that – I used to eat like that. Mars bars, toffees, anything. Anything I could lay my hands on. I got so spotty. I looked like a currant bun – a big, bloated currant bun waddling about stuffed to the ears with sweets and chocolates. Isn't that horrible?'

Tony relaxed for a moment, having captured her eyes more realistically than he thought he would ever ever be capable of.

'People do strange things when they're that sort of age,' he said. 'I remember seeing a cartoon where someone put a pin on someone's seat – Tom and Jerry or something like that, I suppose. I thought it was really funny. I put a drawing-pin on my mum's seat. I got all my toys confiscated for a month.' He laughed shamefacedly. 'You just don't think – do you? You don't think how painful it would be to actually sit on a drawing-pin? You just think of the cartoon – Tom leaping up into the air – howling – and clinging on to the ceiling with all his claws . . .'

'Twelve-year-old kids are all horrible . . .' said Rachel. '. . . I hated being called "fatty" – but it didn't stop me eating. You'd think it would, wouldn't you? You'd think it'd make you vow never to eat again. But it doesn't. It just makes you sneak off and eat even more to try and cheer yourself up. This is a rotten society for being fat in . . .'

'You're not fat now . . .'

'Not *as* fat . . .'

'Not fat at all . . . I don't like skinny girls, anyway.'

'You're just being kind.' She looked at him with her big, glowing, solemn eyes. 'You're the kindest person I know . . .'

Tony shrugged, 'Not really . . .'

'You are. I can't imagine you ever doing anything to hurt anyone.'

'Don't you believe it . . .' Tony's mind flew back. '. . . I did something really hurtful . . . hurtful to you . . . I shouldn't tell you. No, I want to. Look, if I tell you something that I'm really sorry for – that I'd give anything not to have done – if I tell it you, will you promise to forgive me and still like me?'

'Of course.'

'Me and Mog and Chris Harriet – it was Harriet's idea – I'd just got my camera, and Chris said . . .' Gradually, falteringly Tony told Rachel about the photograph that he had taken of her in Annabel Clews's back garden.

Rachel said nothing.

'Are you angry?'

'No,' she smiled. 'No, I'm not angry. Why should you have cared – you hardly knew me then. I was just the blimp that went around with Annabel Clews. I'm used to being laughed at – you do get used to it. You never actually enjoy it – but you learn to ignore it . . . mostly . . . specially when everyone is drooling over Annabel and you're just standing there like a spare zeppelin at a party . . . if only they knew . . .'

'Knew what?'

'Nothing.'

'Anyway, I never drooled over her.'

'You must be the only one, then.'

'I don't even think she's attractive, particularly . . .'

'Don't be daft – she's completely beautiful – sickeningly beautiful . . .'

'No she isn't. She's just chocolate-boxy. Anyway . . . look, I know she's your friend – but . . . that thing she did to Chris Harriet – with the card. That was totally evil.'

'Oh, yes. But you can be beautiful and evil. Like Snow White's stepmother. Perfectly beautiful and horribly cruel. I know Annabel. You don't have to pussyfoot round her for my sake. She can be so vicious when the mood's on her – spiteful. I don't know why. Well . . . I know why she's doing it to your mate Chris – but I can't tell you about that. I don't bother wondering about her any more. It's just Annabel. Take it or leave it. Pure, acidy Annabel . . .'

'That's why I don't think she's beautiful,' said Tony. 'You can't be beautiful – not properly – if you behave like that . . .'

'Maybe . . .'

'Definitely. You're miles beautifuller . . . more beautiful, I mean . . . more beautiful than she is. I'd rather spend my time drawing you than drawing her any day . . .'

'Belladonna . . .' said Rachel. 'She's like Belladonna . . . gorgeous and poisonous. Belladonna Clews. Will you come to my birthday party?'

'Is it your birthday? When?'

'Half-term week. I'm having a party on the Wednesday. I want you to come.'

'I'd like to.'

'Good. Good, good, good.' She smiled broadly. 'Rabbit, rabbit, rabbit . . .'

'What?'

'Rabbit, rabbit, rabbit,' she laughed. 'I'll tell you at the party, maybe. Get on drawing or you'll never finish.'

Tony shrugged and picked up his pencil.

'He said I was beautiful,' said Rachel through a mouthful of muesli. She was reading a letter from her brother.

'What? Ben?'

Rachel looked up. 'No, Tony. Yesterday.'

'I thought you meant Ben had,' said Rebecca. 'I thought he must have gone gaga.'

'I pretended not to notice,' said Rachel, shovelling in another spoonful. 'But I went all gooey inside . . .'

'Don't talk and eat at the same time,' said her father. 'It's like looking into the back of a dust-cart.' With both hands he made the motion of jaws champing.

'What's Ben got to say?' asked Rebecca.

'. . . He'll try to make it for my party. He's in Leeds doing a mural or something for . . . I can't make it out . . . it looks like "for the camel". His writing . . .' Rebecca took the letter.

'For the council, you twit. For the camel! He's doing a big wall painting for the local council. Can't you read?'

'I can read,' said Rachel, 'if he'd learn to write. Anyway, I don't want to talk about him. Did you hear what I said Tony said?'

'That you were beautiful, yes,' said Rebecca. 'You know what *that* means, don't you? That's the first step on the road to sticking his hand up your skirt.'

'Becky!' from Father, tapping her arm with his teaspoon. 'We don't want sex rearing its ugly head at the breakfast table, do we?'

'That's hot,' said Rebecca. The spoon was fresh out of her father's cup of tea.

'Good.'

'He doesn't mean it like that,' said Rachel, through muesli again.

'Rachel! Mouth!'

'Yes. Okay. Sorry. Anyway . . .' she slurped in another spoonful, '. . . he *doesn't* mean it like that. He doesn't mean "cor you're beautiful" like . . . like "cor I want to leap on you" . . .'

'Rachel!' Their father nearly choked on his tea.

'. . . he means it like: "cor that's a beautiful tree" or "cor that's a beautiful building" . . . he doesn't look at me at all, *ever,* the way you're talking about . . . not *sexually* . . .'

'Not much . . .'

In went another spoonful of food. 'I ought to know. It's me he's looking at, isn't it?'

'Rachel, for the last time . . .'

'Ssshh Dad, I'm trying to explain to Becky,' dismissing her father with a wave, 'he doesn't look at me as if I'm a *person*, never mind as if I'm a girl . . .' Neither of them noticed their father get up and walk out '. . . it's so frustrating, sometimes. He's sitting there really staring at me and I'm thinking: Wow . . . if only he was looking at me – me Rachel like that – rather than me a collection of light areas and dark areas and all shades in between . . . but I know he isn't . . .' the front door slammed '. . . and sometimes I stare into his eyes – he's got the loveliest, clearest brown eyes you've ever seen – and I think "you're lovely" over and over again – think it really hard at him – hoping he'll pick it up. "You're lovely . . . you're lovely . . . you're lovely . . ." and he's looking right into my eyes, but I know he's only looking at reflections and shadows . . .'

'Tell him . . .' said Becky, ever practical.

'I can't . . .' said Rachel resignedly.

'Why not?'

'I told you. He doesn't think of me like that. If I start going all soppy it'll muck everything up . . . I know it will. Anyway . . . whenever I get so full of wanting to tell him how I feel that I have to say *something*, I just say "Rabbit!" It's my secret way of telling him that I'm crazy about him without him knowing what it means. Rabbit, rabbit, rabbit . . .'

'It's your funeral . . .' said Rebecca. 'Either you want him or you don't . . .' The telephone rang.

'I don't know that I do want him like that,' said Rachel, reaching for the telephone. 'Well yes . . . I do know I want him like that, really, but . . .' she swallowed and put the receiver to her ear. 'Ronchetti residence?' she said.

'This is your father speaking,' said the familiar voice. 'Will you please stop talking with your mouth full.'

Rachel shrieked with laughter, nearly choking herself in the process, and, helplessly, handed the receiver over to her bemused sister.

Chapter 10

'Parcel for you,' called Tony's father.

Tony appeared at the head of the stairs in pyjama trousers with a toothbrush sticking out of his mouth. 'Whaaa . . .?' he said incoherently, '. . . wussuh . . .?'

'Photographs, it looks like. I'll leave it on the stand.'

'. . .Ogoog . . .' said Tony, vanishing back into the bathroom. And about time too, he thought. The holiday rush must have slowed them down.

If he hadn't been in such a hurry to get to school that Monday morning then the crisis of the birthday party would have been averted. If he hadn't wanted to get into the Art Block before anyone else then he wouldn't have simply shoved the thick packet into his jacket pocket on his way out and Mog and Chris would never have seen the photographs.

As it was, with the parcel in his pocket, and the portrait of Rachel rolled up under his arm, he set off for school a quarter of an hour earlier than usual. Once in the Art Block he pinned up the picture on the section of wall reserved for his work and stood back to admire it. He couldn't help smiling. He couldn't help clutching at his shoulders and shaking with pleasure. It was exactly like Rachel, even down to the strangely pensive way she held her lips, and the way she had of letting her head tilt downwards slightly so that the areas under her eyebrows became the darkest part of her face.

He laughed out loud. 'Even your eyes,' he said. 'I've got you. I've even got your eyes.' It had taken six hours. Tony hadn't finally given up until five o'clock in the evening when the light was beginning to get hazy and he found that, under an electric bulb, every single line on her face looked different. He had had to finish it at home – working through until two o'clock in the morning to complete her hair. Working from memory but managing to negotiate the chaotic tangle of her violently red mane as it splashed thick and sensuous over her shoulders.

He left the block. He had no wish to be caught being narcissistic. He intended just to stroll in later, cool and modest, and pretend it was nothing much.

In the sixth form common room he finally got round to opening the packet of photographs. The one of Rachel was on top. The zoom lens had done its job very well. With only a brief, unhappy glance at it, he pushed the picture into his inside jacket pocket, intending to destroy it.

The other photographs were mostly of Nunhead Cemetery and, of course, at the end, of grandad looking like a lunatic reptile with his mouth full of long and grisly teeth.

Other sixth-formers began to drift in. 'Hello,' said Mog. 'Piccies? Let's look.'

'Is this *those* ones?' asked Chris. 'The ones with the one of Spag Bol?'

'It didn't come out,' said Tony. 'I couldn't have wound the film on far enough.'

'Oh. Pity,' said Chris, 'I was looking forward to seeing that.'

'Let's have a look anyway,' said Mog. Tony handed him the folder of photographs. 'I'll be able to see better by the window,' said Mog, walking off.

'Heard about the party?' Tony asked Chris.

'Party? No. When?'

'P'raps you're not invited . . .' said Tony with a shrug. Behind him Mog was suspiciously holding the negatives of the photographs up to the sunlight. He found the one he was looking for and, with a grin, slipped the strip into his pocket.

'What party's this?' he asked, coming back.

'Rachel Ronchetti's birthday party – but I don't know if you're invited. She only told me yesterday . . .'

'Yesterday?' said Chris. 'Where d'you see her yesterday?'

'We were doing some stuff together,' said Tony evasively, 'work. For art.'

'. . . Really . . .?' said Chris.

'Art, eh?' said Mog, waggling his eyebrows. 'Artistic poses, eh? Nudge, nudge . . . *artistic* poses, eh?'

'Prat,' said Tony.

Chris was intrigued. 'You doing pictures of each other, then?'

'We do,' said Tony, 'but we don't, repeat, don't do the sort of artistic poses Mog is talking about . . .'

'I haven't said a sausage,' said Mog, spreading his hands out. 'What have I said?'

'Do you see a lot of Spag Bol, then?' asked Chris.

'In art, yes – a bit.'

Chris frowned thoughtfully. 'She's The Clews's best mate, isn't she?'

'I suppose . . .'

'So The Clews'll be at the party, won't she . . .?'

Tony shrugged.

'So if you can wangle me an invite . . .'

'And me,' said Mog. 'Don't forget me . . .'

'Wangle *us* an invite, then . . . I'll be able to prove to The Clews what a brilliant catch I am.'

'Hang on,' said Tony. 'You want me to get Rachel to invite you so that you can have another go at The Clews? Is that the idea?'

'Got it,' said Chris.

'Go on,' said Mog. 'Use your privileged position. Get us

invited.'

'What's in it for you?' Tony asked Mog.

Mog pointed at Chris. 'Amusement value,' he said. 'It's been a bit quiet since the little love letter . . .'

'I've telephoned her,' said Chris.

'Where d'you get her number?'

'Out of the book. Where d'you think?'

'What happened?' asked Mog.

'I phoned up, right? On Friday evening. Some woman answered – her mum I suppose – and I said, "It's a friend of Annabel's, is she in, please?" Note the "please" – dead polite. "Yes," she said, "just a moment." This is it, I thought, keep calm, Harriet – suave and sophisticated. Anyway, she came to the phone. "Hello," she said, in that *voice* of hers. "It's Chris Harriet," I said. "I was wondering if you were doing anything special tonight?" There was a pause then she said, "Wait while I look in my diary." I might have known . . .'

'Known what?' asked Tony.

'Well . . . she put the phone down and I thought she'd gone to check her diary. Bloody fool, I was – as if anyone would have to check their diary to see what they were doing that night . . .'

'So?' said Mog.

'. . . so nothing. I sat there clutching the receiver for ten minutes – waiting for her to come back – like a right flippin' berk . . .'

'And she never did . . .' said Mog.

'And she never did. I hung up and tried again but it was engaged. She'd left it off the hook. If she thinks she's going to put me off that easily she's wrong.'

'Persistent little sod, aren't you?' said Tony.

Chris made a sweeping gesture with his arm. 'Where The Clews is concerned, nothing is too much effort. I'd walk barefoot to Siberia for one touch of her . . .' Mog coughed loudly. Chris looked round.

Annabel had just walked in. Minus Rachel.

She came up to Tony. 'Message for you,' she said. 'Rachel said to tell you she's in the Art Room if you're interested.'

'Oh. Ta.' Tony stood up. He tried not to look too eager. 'I might as well wander over there, I suppose.'

'You might as well,' said Mog, deadpan.

'Did you find out whether you were busy Friday night?' Chris asked Annabel.

She looked at him. 'Don't you ever take no for an answer?'

'I'm making an exception in your case . . .'

She walked off. 'Child,' she said over her shoulder.

'She loves me really,' murmured Chris. Tony cast his eyes up at the ceiling in despair and walked out.

'Never mind about that,' said Mog, pulling Chris near to the window. 'Look what I've got.' He drew out the negative strip. 'It's the first one, look.'

Chris held it up to the light. The picture didn't make a lot of sense in reversed colours but it was obvious enough that it was the photograph that Tony had taken of Rachel hunched up on the sun-lounger.

'He said it hadn't come out . . .' said Chris.

'Well,' said Mog, 'they're pals now, aren't they?' He grinned. 'Did you know you can get photoposters made up from negatives like this?'

'Photoposters?'

Mog nodded. 'Imagine it. A blow-up thirty inches by twenty . . .'

Chris grinned. 'That would be priceless . . . a poster of her on the wall . . . in here . . .'

'Better still,' said Mog, '. . . at the party.'

'At the party!' breathed Chris. 'My God, Mog, you're a genius. Can we get it done in time?'

'I'll send it off today. Won't it be a nice surprise for her?'

'Won't it just . . .'

Rachel came running up as Tony walked into the Art Room and for a wonderful, hair-raising moment, he thought she was going to cuddle him. But she stopped dead half a foot away, beaming. 'You're brilliant,' she said, eyes shining. 'It's absolutely marvellous. Everyone's going crazy over it. Mr Treeves is having kittens. Come on.'

Treeves stood in a gaggle of students, all looking with rapt attention at the drawing. Treeves put his hand on Tony's shoulder. 'You've done it, Anthony,' he said.

Tony grinned, basking in the general effusions of praise.

'How did you do it?'

'How on earth long did it take?'

'I couldn't draw like that in a million years.'

'What pencils did you use?'

'Did you have to use an eraser?'

Tony enjoyed the attention, and Rachel was content just to stand on the sidelines, receiving a share of reflected glory.

'It's magnificent,' said Treeves at last. 'I can hardly criticise it at all.' He scratched at his beard. 'But I must . . . I must . . .' He moved in closer. 'Yes.' He indicated the sweep of her hair. 'This isn't quite right, is it? Close, but not quite. Was it done at a different time? The light doesn't hit it quite right. See what I mean?' He indicated a few areas. 'See?'

Tony nodded, coming gently down to earth.

And I think you could separate the tones a little.' Treeves indicated a fraction with his fingers. 'Just ease them out a tiny bit. Know what I mean?'

'Yes.' Tony wasn't sure he did, but all the praise had made him feel like a real artist for the first time and he didn't want to ruin it by not knowing what 'separate the tones a little' meant. He could always ask Rachel later.

'Okay, bonnie babies, to work, to work . . .' said Treeves. The gathering dispersed. 'By the bye – the National Gallery?'

Tony opened his mouth.

'We're going tonight,' said Rachel quickly. 'There wasn't time over the weekend, was there?' She looked at Tony. 'Was there? It took all weekend to do this.' Meaning the picture.

'Okay,' said Treeves. 'Stay of execution. But be sure you go tonight. I want a full report.'

Tony and Rachel went to their tables. They had drawing-boards already set up and were in the middle of a number of sketches of a chair which Treeves had hung from a ceiling beam. 'Draw the spaces,' he had said. 'Draw the gaps. I want to see you looking right *through* it, really understanding the geometry. Go to it . . .'

'You are a clever thing,' said Rachel as they sat at their drawing-boards.

Tony smiled. 'Drawing you is easy,' he said, 'you've got such an interesting face . . .'

Interesting! thought Rachel. You told me I was beautiful yesterday. Tell me I'm beautiful again!

'Will the gallery be open tonight?' asked Tony.

''Til seven,' said Rachel. 'We can get a number twelve to Trafalgar Square. I know the way.'

'That's good – I don't.'

'Haven't you *ever* been there?'

Tony shook his head.

'You're hopeless. How many galleries have you been to?'

'Approximately?' asked Tony.

'Yes.'

'Approximately . . . er . . . none.'

'Right,' said Rachel, 'let's make a deal. I'll do you the gallery tour – all the ones you ought to have been to *years* ago – and in return you sit for me to do a portrait of you?'

'Deal,' said Tony.

Rachel nodded. Now she would have him to herself for some evenings as well.

They were sitting in front of a large, complicated painting by Rubens.

'*Minerva Protects Pax from Mars*,' read Rachel from their guide leaflet. It was one of those rich, full-bodied old paintings full of cherubs and satyrs and plump people doing odd things. There was even a leopard rolling about on the floor and right in the middle, to Tony's affront, sat a thick-limbed and round-bellied woman squirting milk from her breast into the mouth of a nearby infant.

'They had some funny ideas . . .' said Tony.

'That's Pax – the woman giving the milk – nurturing Plutus, the god of wealth. See? Peace feeding Wealth? That chap in the armour is the god of war, and he's being kept away by Minerva . . .'

'Who was she, then?'

'I don't know. It doesn't say. It's all to do with things being better when there's not a war . . .'

'Yes. Well, that doesn't take a lot of working out . . .'

They looked at the picture in silence for a while.

'Let's not try to look at *everything*,' Rachel had said as they had climbed the steps inside the front entrance. 'My poor little legs won't stand it.'

'You choose, then.' There was a map of the main areas. Rachel had plotted a route beginning with the Italians and ending with the French Impressionists. The Dutch Masters were all brown, dark and gloomy. '. . . Chiaroscuro . . .' Rachel had said. 'Oh,' Tony had replied, clueless. The Italians went for plump women a lot – lounging about in the countryside or doing things with gods and fat babies. The first things that Tony really liked were the Turner sunsets on pictures like *The Fighting Temeraire*. But the Impressionists had been a real revelation – especially Seurat's *La Baignade, Asnières* and Degas's painting, all done in shades of red, of one woman combing out another's hair.

After their tour they had wandered into the shop and Rachel had bought a few postcards. Tony had wanted a poster of the Seurat – but it was too expensive. They had come out of the shop and found themselves a red plush seat so that Rachel – who had been right about her legs – could have a rest.

'Do you think all the women were that shape in those days?' asked Tony.

'Skinniness is quite a recent fashion –' said Rachel. 'In

those days it was the "in" thing to be big – it meant you could afford to eat – that you had plenty of money. Only poor people and ill people were thin. All the fatties were rolling in money. It was a sort of status symbol, I suppose, to have a huge gut . . .'

'It's the other way round now . . .'

'Yes.'

'Pity,' said Tony. Rachel looked quizzically at him. 'I mean, well . . .' Tony wasn't sure what he had meant. 'They look . . . all . . . sort of . . . grabbable . . . you know . . .?'

'Not really. Grabbable?'

'No, not grabbable . . . I didn't mean that . . . I meant . . . warm. They look warm – as if they'd be nice to hold . . .'

'Like big hot-water bottles . . .'

'Yes. Well, something like that . . .' Tony's next question, in that context, was the height of tactlessness. 'Would you pose like that – with nothing on?'

'No.'

He smiled. 'Me neither.' He did not realise that he had offended her. I've lost nearly a stone for you, she was thinking, and you more or less tell me I look like some fat woman out of a Rubens painting!

'Cold, I should imagine,' he continued blithely. 'Not to mention uncomfortable . . .'

It was a few minutes before Tony began to suspect that her silence was more than simply having nothing to say.

'You okay?'

'No, not really.'

'What is it?'

'I've got a pain.'

'Where?'

'Don't ask.'

Tony looked puzzled. 'Headache?'

'No,' she pressed her hand against her abdomen. 'Lower.'

'Can I do anything?'

'No. It's all right. It's nothing unusual. It'll go away in a minute.' But it didn't. The cramps got gradually worse, like someone shoving a hand in through her abdomen and squeezing spitefully. She leaned forwards, holding herself.

Tony felt acutely embarrassed. If she kept this up people were going to notice. He wished for a second that he could simply get up and leave her to it. How on earth was he going to get her home? Why did it have to happen to him? At least she could have pretended not to be in pain until she was at her own house where her mother could deal with it. If Mog or Chris got gut-ache you could just tell them it served them right or you could have a debate about what they'd eaten that might have caused it . . .

'Have you eaten something funny?' offered Tony tentatively.

'It's my period,' said Rachel, just managing not to add – you stupid bastard!

Tony felt like someone pushed out of an aeroplane halfway across the Atlantic.

It was a long time before he unscrambled his brain sufficiently to touch her shoulder gingerly and say 'Sorry . . .'

She looked round at him. 'What are you being sorry for – you're not doing anything,' she snapped. It was the first time he had ever touched her and she had been too preoccupied to notice.

He took his hand away – feeling stupid.

The pain eased slightly and she sat up. 'I'm going home,' she said. 'I don't know what you're doing.'

The journey home was undertaken in tense silence. Rachel was wrapped in her pain as though in a blanket of barbed wire and Tony felt both upset and unwelcome. He began to wonder if it might have been more sensible to have left her at the bus stop as she had suggested.

He stood at the gate. As she put the key in the lock she glanced round. He looked so thin and sad and lost that she felt a rush of remorse. 'Come in for some coffee . . .' she said.

He hesitated. She held out her hand. 'Please . . .'

The house was quiet and empty. They sat in the kitchen.

'Would you like something to eat?' she asked. 'We haven't got a lot in – tomorrow's shopping day – but I can probably find an egg or two . . .'

'No, thanks.'

'Dad always shops on Tuesday,' said Rachel, looking in the fridge. 'He goes to night school Wednesday and on Thursday and Friday the supermarket's always full of pensioners and dole people who've just got their cheques. It must be horrible having to wait for money to come through the post.'

'It is if it's late,' said Tony. 'Mog's dad's on the dole. If the cheque doesn't come they don't eat that night. It's as tight as that on the money they get. They can just afford to get by – but if the cheque's delayed they're completely banjaxed.'

'I didn't know that about Mog,' said Rachel. 'How long's that been?'

'Six months, I think. He was a trade union activist. There was a strike or something and he got sacked. I don't know much about it – Mog doesn't talk about it.'

'Why's he called Mog?'

'It's short for Morgan.'

'I thought his name was Alton . . .'

'It is. Morgan Alton. Mog for short.'

'Oh. I thought it was short for "moggy". You know – moggy: catty. Catty because he's always being so catty – sarcastic.'

'I'll tell him that . . .'

'No, don't.' Rachel sat down at the table opposite Tony, twirling her coffee mug round and round in her hands. 'He's the one who started calling me Spag Bol, isn't he?' Tony looked anxiously at her. 'Wasn't I supposed to know about that?' she said.

'I don't call you that,' said Tony.

'Not now,' said Rachel softly. 'You used to, though. I've heard you.'

'It doesn't mean anything – it's just your name . . .

Ronchetti – rhymes with spaghetti – spaghetti bolognese – Spag Bol.'

Rachel looked up. 'Oh. I didn't make the connection. I thought it was something to do with me looking like a plate of spaghetti bolognese, or something . . .'

Tony laughed. 'How could anyone look like a plate of spaghetti bolognese?'

'I don't know. I'm just used to being insulted about how I look, I suppose. I'm just paranoid. Don't worry about it.'

'I don't know why . . .' said Tony, '. . . you look all right to me.'

'So what's all right?' said Rachel with a shrug.

'I think you're very attractive,' said Tony, seriously. 'Honest.'

'Like St Paul's . . .'

'What?'

'Forget it.'

'Have I annoyed you?'

'No.' She pulled an apologetic face. 'No. It's not you. My gut still hurts and I'm feeling ratty. Take no notice.'

'You know that photograph I told you about – the one of you in Annabel Clews's back garden?'

'Yes.'

'It came this morning – through the post.'

'Oh . . .'

'I told the others it hadn't come out . . .'

'Had it?'

'Yes.' He felt in his jacket pocket. 'It's here. I haven't looked at it – honest – I haven't even looked at it. I'll tear it up.'

'No. Let me see.'

He handed the photograph over. It was an appallingly uncomplimentary pose. Rachel felt herself going red and prickly. Plonked, hunched over in the middle of the lounger – legs splayed all over the place – stomach creased into rolls like pink tyres, and she was painting her toenails – she looked utterly revolting and she was painting her bloody toe-nails!

'I haven't looked at it,' said Tony again, shaking his head.

Rachel slowly tore the photograph into tiny pieces, saying nothing.

'I'm sorry,' said Tony. 'I'll go and cut my throat, shall I?'

A single tear rolled down her cheek.

'Go away,' she said huskily.

'Rachel . . .'

'Just go away, Tony, please . . .'

She didn't let herself cry properly until she heard the front door click behind him, but then she threw her head forwards into her arms and sobbed and sobbed until her whole body ached with it.

The telephone rang. Tony, curled into a ball in an armchair, ignored it. Only Chris and Mog ever telephoned for him and he didn't much want to speak to either of them. Anyway, it was probably for Mum or Dad, or some twitty girl phoning to talk to Martin who was everyone's flavour of the month at the moment. Fourteen years old, Martin – and a sex life like something out of a teen magazine. Incredible.

Martin ran in. 'Hell-oo? Hot-lips speaking.' A pause while whoever was on the other end of the phone came to terms with this introduction. 'What?' He threw the receiver on to the arm of Tony's chair. 'For you,' he said.

It was Rachel.

'Tony?'

'Yes.' Should he be sullen and hurt, or glad to hear from her? After all, she had told him to go away not an hour ago.

'It's me . . .'

'Hello, me . . .'

'Hello.' There was a daft silence. 'You still there?'

'Yes,' said Tony. 'How's your tummy?'

'Not so bad. I've taken some paracetamol. I feel like a wretch . . . Can I see you?'

'Of course.'

'Now?' asked Rachel.

'Yes. Where?'

'I don't know.'

'Shall I come round?'

'No. Somewhere else. Somewhere outdoors.'

'How about Nunhead Cemetery? I could meet you there – by the main entrance. It's nice there.'

'Yes. I know. Opposite the church, you mean? I know where . . .'

'What sort of time, then?'

'Soon . . .'

'Soon as you like, I'm not up to anything here.'

'Ten minutes?'

'Fine.'

'Can I bring some drawing stuff? I'd like to do some sketches of you . . . is that okay?'

Tony had a quick wash, changed his clothes and ran all the way. Rachel was already there, a pad and pencil case under her arm. She had been out of the front door almost before the telephone receiver had hit the cradle.

'What would you like for your birthday?' asked Tony. He was lying full length in the grass with his hands behind his head. Rachel was sitting cross-legged in a foam of skirt, sketching briskly. She did it with an almost unconscious flair, dashing off lines at a great pace – every touch of the charcoal making a mark that would have taken Tony, with his pains-taking, blood-sweating style, an age to get right. Generally, he loved to watch the fluidity of her approach – but now he was staring up into the ceramic blue sky and just enjoying being the object of her work.

'A surprise,' she said.

'What sort of surprise?'

'A surprising sort of surprise.'

'I can't think of anything surprising . . .'

'Oh, I don't mind. Just give me you,' said Rachel lightly.

She was quite relieved that she had made it sound like a joke.

'Gift-wrapped,' said Tony, 'with a little ribbon.'

'Rabbit!' shouted Rachel. Tony looked round, startled. 'What?'

'Rabbit . . .' said Rachel in her normal voice. She twitched her shoulders. 'I have to say it every now and then or I'll go mad.'

'What does it mean?'

'It's a secret.'

'Even from me?'

'Especially from you.'

Tony frowned. 'You're very puzzling, sometimes,' he said.

'Rabbit!' she said, smiling. She widened her eyes and stared intently at him. 'Rabbit.'

'Rabbit back,' he said. 'Is that right? Rabbit back and doubled?'

'But it's not true!' she said vehemently, throwing the drawing-pad aside and getting to her feet. 'You don't *mean* it!'

'I don't know what it means,' said Tony, kneeling up. 'Rachel!'

'It's okay,' she said, sitting down again. 'All over. Tea in a stormcup.'

'Eh?'

'It's Ronchetti speak: storm in a teacup. Don't worry about it.'

Tony knelt on his heels, looking anxiously at her.

She smiled, reaching for the drawing-pad. 'Hold that pose,' she said, 'it makes you look sweet.'

'You're totally loopy.'

'Look who's talking.'

'Oh . . . rabbit!' said Tony.

'Don't,' said Rachel, her face strangely serious. 'Not until you mean it.'

She was, he thought, completely and utterly loopy.

Chapter 11

'Perhaps he's gay,' said Rebecca.

'Don't be sick,' said Rachel, horrified.

'Who's sick? People are, you know. It's not unheard of.'

'Tony isn't like that. You have got a nasty mind, sometimes.'

'What's nasty about it? I didn't think you were like that about gays.'

'I'm not, of course I'm not. I didn't mean . . .'

'That's typical,' said Rebecca, confronting Rachel. 'Gut reaction!'

'Oh, shut up.'

They carried on flicking through the racks of clothes. It was the first Saturday of half-term and Rachel had dragged her sister out to help find a new outfit for the party.

Rachel pulled out a flouncy white skirt. 'How 'bout this?'

'No,' said Rebecca firmly.

'What's wrong with it?'

'It'll make you look ten pounds heavier again. Wait until you're really skinny, then you can wear white.'

'What are we looking for, then?'

'Something dark – black preferably.'

'I want skirt and top separate,' said Rachel. 'Not a dress.'

'I know. I've already thought about a top. Something with a big, loose neck so it can sort of hang off one shoulder and look all come-hither. Oooh, look . . .' She pulled out a long black skirt with thick, voluptuous folds. 'Try that.'

They crammed into a changing booth.

'You don't really think he's . . . the other way . . . do you?' asked Rachel, unzipping her jeans. 'Not really . . .'

'Why don't you ask him?'

'I couldn't. It'd be so embarrassing.'

'You are a nit. I'll ask him if you like – at the party.'

'Don't you dare.' She stepped out of her jeans and took the skirt out of her sister's hands.

'Does it matter?'

'Of course it matters.'

'Why?'

'You know . . . you know I'm completely batty about him. What's the point in wasting all this . . . this *passion*, only to find out he's having it away with Mog Alton or someone . . .'

'Mog?'

'Skip it.' Rachel pulled the skirt up over her hips and buttoned the waist. 'What do you think?' she asked, regarding her profile in the mirror.

'Not bad . . .' said Rebecca.

'Does it make me look thin?'

'Of course not, but with the right sort of top it should make you look dead sexy, I reckon. You want a top that'll sort of fall open when you go forward – you know – so you can lean over your Tony-bloke when you give him a drink and he'll be able to see all the way down to your navel. That's the best test of if a bloke's gay or not – a quick flash of cleavage.'

'I haven't got any cleavage,' said Rachel. 'Not unless I go like this . . .' she pushed her arms forward and towards each other, '. . . and I can't go about like that all night. He'll think I'm deformed. I'll have to get a special bra – one that'll shove them together . . .'

'You don't want a bra, that's not part of the masterplan — mistress-plan, I should say.'

'I'm not marching about without my foundation wear,' said Rachel in a mock-prudish, spinsterly voice. 'Whatever next!'

'You're so inhibited,' said Rebecca. 'No wonder Tony doesn't realise you fancy him.'

'I can't help it.' Rachel's face dissolved into misery. 'Oh, Becky, what am I going to do?'

Rebecca became very efficient. 'We're going to make you so desirable that the moment Tony sees you he'll just jump on you, that's what we're going to do.'

'And what if he doesn't?'

'Then you'll have to jump on him . . . I can't understand why you don't anyway . . . I would if I fancied someone that much.'

'Would you?'

'Rachel, listen . . .'

'No,' Rachel took the skirt off. 'I'll sort it out. Don't worry.'

'Get drunk,' said Rebecca, 'Believe me — just get drunk. That'll sort everything out . . . one way or another . . .'

'Rabbit (rae bit)n.,pl.-bits. 1. any of various common gregarious burrowing leporid mammals, esp. *Oryctolagus cuniculus* of Europe and North Africa and the cottontail of America. 2. the fur of such an animal. 3. Brit. informal, a novice or poor performer at a game or sport. — vb.(intr.) 4. to hunt or shoot rabbits. 5. (often foll. by on or away) Brit. slang. to talk inconsequentially; chatter. (14th cent. perhaps from Walloon *robett*, diminutive of Flemish *robbe* rabbit, of obscure origin).'

Tony closed the dictionary. 'Six,' he said to himself, 'word used by Rachel Ronchetti to confuse Tony Anderson. Meaning unknown.' He slid the book back under the side-unit and wandered into the hall. Sounds of Mother from kitchen. Dad was doing something to the car – as usual. The day would come when that car would be so perfect that there was nothing to be tinkered with – on that day Tony imagined that his father would simply cease to exist, his role in life having been fulfilled.

Five days to the party. Four if you didn't include today. No present yet.

Tony went upstairs. Grandad was confined to bed again. He had never really got over the cold he'd had last month and in the last two days he had gone so wheezy and shaky that Tony's mother had put him to bed. Like you would a small child. 'Off to bed, my lad – I'll bring you up a drink later. Nice hot lemon . . .'

Tony knocked and opened the door.

Grandad was reading the newspaper. The room smelt odd. Unpleasant.

'Laddo,' said Grandad, 'got me some tea?'

'I can do,' said Tony. 'I want some advice.'

'Tea first – then sympathy. That's the order of things. Tea first.'

Tony made a pot of tea and brought the tray up to his grandad's room.

He sat on the edge of the bed. There were screwed up tissues everywhere. 'Two things,' said Tony.

'Fire away.'

'Do you know if "rabbit" means anything apart from the obvious? I've looked in the dictionary – Rachel keeps saying "rabbit" to me, but she won't tell me what it means. It definitely means something very particular – but I can't suss out what and she won't tell me . . .'

Grandad scratched his front teeth thoughtfully, like a tyrannosaurus picking bits of pterodactyl out of its fangs after dinner. 'Does she mean you talk too much?'

'No. I'm sure it's not that.'

'P'raps she's telling you you're a weed . . . feeble . . .'

'I don't think it's that, either. I hope not, anyway.'

Grandad blew his nose marshily and another tissue joined the conglomeration. 'You know what rabbits are famous for, don't you?'

'Eating carrots?'

'Breeding.'

'Breeding?'

'Breed like rabbits. You must know that one. Breeding like rabbits.'

'Oh, I see . . .' said Tony with heavy irony. 'She's telling me she wants to breed with me, is that it? Thanks, Grandad, I really hadn't thought of that one.'

'Mark my words . . .'

'I should breeding-well think so . . .'

'That's my opinion.'

'Ta.'

'Is that it? Can I get back to me paper?'

'Yes. Get back to your breeding paper. No – hold on – there's something else. I need a present-idea for her birthday – for Rachel's birthday . . .'

'Ask your mum . . .'

'No. She'll just say get something practical . . . like a dish-cloth or a bag of pegs . . .'

'True,' said Grandad reflectively. 'She never was what you'd call a romantic, your mother. I remember when . . .'

'You must be able to think of something,' said Tony, in no mood for a ramble down his grandfather's memory lane.

'Does she wear jewellery?'

Tony thought for a moment. 'No,' he said, '. . . oh . . . hold on . . . she wears a necklace sometimes. A little, thin gold one.'

'There you are . . . get her a necklace . . . get her a nice necklace . . . now push off, I want to read me paper . . .'

'Owww!'

'Don't be such a baby.' Her mother had Rachel's head firmly under one arm, as if she was holding a pudding basin.

'Stop blinking, you twit, or I'll never get it.'

'Careful . . .' Rachel's eyes were streaming and her nose was snivelly.

'You don't half look funny . . .' said her mother.

'I'm glad someone's enjoying this.'

'It's your own fault,' said Rebecca, leaning over to try and see what was going on. 'You know you're supposed to take them out at night.' The new contact lenses were proving troublesome.

'I forgot.'

'Get out of the light, Becky. I can't see a thing with you looming all over the place.'

Their father was rummaging in the cupboard under the sink. 'Ha!' he said, 'Here we are!' He displayed a sink-plunger. 'Will this help?'

'Don't make me laugh, Dad, its . . . owww!'

'Got it.' said her mother triumphantly.

Rachel was released. She ground her knuckles into her puffy, red-rimmed eyes. 'They hurt!' she wailed plaintively, blinking myoptically at her mother.

'You shouldn't have left them in so long. You'll get used to them.'

'By Wednesday?' said Rachel, examining her face in the mirror on the inside lid of the lens case. 'Oh, God, I look like I've been in a boxing match. It's only two days to go.'

'Put them in at the last minute and take them out straight away afterwards,' said her mother. 'You'll be all right.'

'I'd better be.'

'How much weight have you lost now?' asked Rebecca.

'A stone and a half,' said Rachel, exaggerating slightly.

'That's good,' said her mother.

'Fancy a sausage?' asked her father.

'No.'

'Special slimming sausages . . .'

'No!' Rachel stood up, pulling her dressing gown round herself. 'What have you decided . . . for the party?'

'You mean where are we going to hide ourselves?' asked her mother.

'Aren't we coming?' asked her father.

'No. You're not.'

'Don't fret. We're spending the night at Brian's place. It's all sorted out. We shan't be in the way.'

'Good.'

'It's not just for your benefit,' said her mother. 'I don't fancy a night of your boom-boom music. Have you warned the neighbours?'

'Yes.'

'You can borrow some of my records if you like . . .' said her father.

'No thanks. I don't think The Incredible String Band will go down all that well . . .'

Her father made an offended noise. 'Be like that.'

'Are you getting excited yet?' asked Rebecca.

'Yes.' Rachel bounced on her toes. 'Yes. But Wednesday's so far away. What have you got me, Mum? Eh? Eh? What have you got me?'

'Contact lenses.'

'Yes, but what else . . .'

'You gold-digger . . .'

'I've got to have something to open on the day . . .' said Rachel.

'We've got you a box of chocolates,' said her father. '. . . a one and a half stone box of chocolates.'

'Thing!' said Rachel. 'Horrible *thing*!'

'Is Tony getting you anything? asked Rebecca.

'He'd better . . .'

'Any idea?'

'He's not said. Knowing him it'll be something to do with art – a box of pencils or something.'

'Who said romance was dead?' said her father.

'I don't know. Do you want me to look it up?'

Rachel sighed. 'I hope he gets me something dead soppy.'

'I'm sure he will,' said Rebecca.
'I'm sure he won't,' said Rachel.

Tony stood gazing into the jeweller's shop window. He had never even thought about jewellery before – never mind actually having to try and pick something to buy. He had a full wallet and an empty head. He stared at the display and the display winked back. There was no avoiding it. With a deep breath, and deeper misgivings he went in.

'I want a necklace.' It was like going into a butcher's shop and saying: 'I've come in for some meat.'

The woman behind the counter was very helpful. She treated Tony like an idiot, which got it about right – gradually extracting from him how much money he wanted to spend, whether he wanted gold or silver – a pendant?

'Yes, that's a good idea.' A few trays were brought out. The range of different coloured stones dazzled him.

'What colouring is she?'

'Sort of pink,' said Tony brainlessly, 'skin colour . . .'

'Her hair.' Patience being a virtue.

'Red,' he made a broad, cupping gesture, 'loads of it – all curly and bouncy . . .'

'What about a tiger's-eye?'

'Eh?'

The stop assistant drew up a slender golden chain. A golden-brown stone hung, like a huge teardrop, from its centre.

Tony smiled. He felt a shiver of delight down his spine as he imagined placing it around Rachel's neck. It would be an excuse to touch her as well – actually touch her skin. 'Yes,' he said. 'That's it. That'll do.'

Chapter 12

'Keep still or it'll go in your eye.'

'Sorry.' Rachel endeavoured to hold her head still while Annabel applied eyeliner.

'Look up,' said Annabel.

'I am looking up . . .'

'Well, look more up, then. Yes . . . that's it. Got it.' A thin black line all round the inside lids. 'That'll make your eyes look huge – absolutely hoo-oooge . . .'

Rachel stared, wide-eyed at herself. 'Oh yes . . .' she said. Even half made up the effect was startling.

'Bit of mascara . . .' said Annabel. Rachel sat quiescent while Annabel fussed over her.

'What about having your hair up?'

'I don't know . . .'

Annabel drew back two thick tangles of hair. 'Like that.'

'It makes me look all cheeks . . . like an Eskimo . . .'

'I'll sort that out in a minute with a bit of blusher . . . I think it'll look good. Just these two side bits brought up and back and tied with a thick velvety sort of ribbon. A big black bow . . . what do you think?'

'I don't know . . .'

'I do. It'll be smashing. Trust me.'

Rachel gave way.

'Is Joe coming down?' she asked.

'Yes – specially. He's catching the five o'clock from Cambridge so he should be here sort of mid to late eveningish.'

'So we get to see him at last. That'll be nice.'

Annabel worked on Rachel in silence for a while.

Rachel nibbled her top lip. 'He's at the university there, isn't he?'

'Yes.'

'What's he taking?'

Their eyes met in the mirror.

'He's not a student . . .' she said, looking away. 'He's a lecturer.'

'Oh . . .'

The entire session took over an hour.

'Right,' said Annabel, at last. 'Look.'

Rachel gazed into the mirror. 'Wow . . .' she breathed, '. . . that's me . . .'

'The new you. This year's Ronchetti – hot off the press. Pleased?'

'I'm gorgeous!'

'You are!' Annabel laughed.

'He must fall in love with me now . . .'

'Absolutely.'

'Wow . . .'

The plan worked perfectly. As Tony came into the hall Rachel was just walking down the stairs.

He stood staring at her.

Annabel and Rebecca were standing in the kitchen doorway. '. . . Hit by a thunderbolt,' whispered Rebecca.

There were already a few people wandering about with drinks.

'Hello,' said Rachel. Shy. Very nervous.

Tony just stood there as though he couldn't believe his eyes.

'Say something, you berk . . .' hissed Annabel out of ear-shot.

But he didn't need to say anything. The look on his face was enough for Rachel. And as for Tony himself – he felt as though he was just melting down out of his clothes and into a sticky pool on the hall carpet.

He held out his present. Wrapped in golden paper.

Rachel took it – her face radiantly happy. She sucked in and nibbled her top lip. 'What is it?'

'Open it.'

'Coats are going in Ben's old room, come on up, I'll show you.' Tony followed her up the stairs. She particularly wanted to be alone with him for a few moments – while she opened his present. She had the feeling it wasn't pencils.

No one took very much notice of Mog and Chris when they arrived, except:

'Oh God . . .' said Annabel, and disappeared into the kitchen in search of the wine box.

Mog had the photoposter rolled up under his jacket. He was planning to save it for a dramatic moment later on during the evening – when everyone was drunk enough to appreciate it. He managed to slide it behind an armchair in the front room, and then the two of them went in search of alcohol.

Tony and Rachel were holding each other so tightly that they could hardly breathe. They had come so naturally into each other's arms that neither of them had had the time to think about it.

'It's lovely . . .' she said, looking up at him with big, solemn eyes, her fingertips just touching the pendant – glowing between them.

'It was just an excuse to cuddle you . . .' said Tony.

'You didn't need an excuse.'

'I wish I'd brought my camera. You look . . .' he gazed at her, melting all over, '. . . fabulous . . .'

'So do you.'

'I want to kiss you, but I don't want to muck up your lipstick . . .'

'I should care . . .'

Rebecca opened the front door yet again. 'Ben!' Tall, thin, bird's-nest hair and denims.

'Me!' said Ben. 'Where's Sis?'

'Upstairs. We thought you'd be here hours ago.'

'I had to hitch. It's a long way. Got any money?'

'You haven't brought anything to drink . . .'

'There's always something with you,' said Ben.

'You could've brought a can at least . . .'

'Don't go on.' He brandished a plain grey box about four inches square. 'I've brought a present.'

'Not wrapped. As usual.'

'Money, Ronchetti Minor, money . . .'

'I've never met *anyone* . . .'

'Cornell!' shouted Ben over his sister's head.

'Benjamin! Well met! There's a polypin of beer in the kitchen. Get in quick while there's still some glasses.'

'Here,' said Ben, thrusting the box into Rebecca's hands. 'Give it to Minimus when she turns up – I've got to go and chat to Cornell . . .'

The doorbell went before Rebecca had a chance to do anything, and by the time she'd let another gang of guests in, Benjamin and Cornell were draped over the polypin, chattering away like monkeys.

Rachel and Tony didn't stay upstairs long – the continuous traffic of people bearing, mostly, coats and, occasionally, presents made any attempts at further intimacy impossible after their first kiss. Tony found Mog and Chris in the kitchen while Rachel did the rounds, showing off both herself and the necklace.

The music was turned up so that conversation in the front room was impossible and people began to drift into the hall and kitchen and dining room to chat, leaving the front room to dancers and the usual scattering of wallflowers.

'Which of these are vegetable?' asked Lucy, their mother's younger sister, hovering over samosas.

'Does it matter?' asked Mog, his paper plate piled with a pyramid of food gleaned from every plate on the table.

'I'm a vegetarian,' said Lucy.

'Yeah?' Mog shook his head. 'I couldn't stand that ... have a sausage roll ...'

Chris had cornered Annabel. He had found her talking to an older man – a man in his late thirties or forties with a lean, lined face and greying hair. Chris assumed, without thinking, that he was someone's uncle or father.

He noticed the way the older man was looking at her and felt slightly disgusted. As Chris pushed forwards the man stepped back with raised eyebrows and an amused smile.

'You look nice,' Chris told Annabel.

'Do I?' she said, looking straight through him.

'Want another drink?'

She displayed a half-full glass to him.

'Dance?'

'No.'

'Don't you like dancing?'

Tiredly. 'Yes.'

'Why don't you want to dance, then?'

Silence.

'Why don't you want to dance, then?'

'If I dance with you will you do something for me?'

'Sure. What?'

She drank and put her glass down.

'Drop dead?'

Rebecca was dancing with her boyfriend, Steven. They were both plump and their dancing mostly consisted of ricocheting off everyone else in the room like a couple of hyperactive billiard balls.

More rings at the front door. The place was getting nicely crowded. Rachel sat on the stairs and opened her present from Ben. It was an ink-pad and a rubber stamp. She dabbed the stamp on the pad and pressed it on to the back of an envelope.

PROPERTY OF RACHEL RONCHETTI

She laughed. Ben always thought of peculiar presents.

The telephone rang. With the receiver pressed against one ear and her hand against the other, Rachel answered it.

'This is the Chief Police Commissioner of London speaking,' said a familiar voice. 'There's going to be a raid . . .'

'Hello, Dad, what do you want?'

'Nothing. I just felt like interrupting the orgy. I'm bored and Brian's droning on about deep-sea fishing. How's it going?'

Rachel held the receiver out to the noise.

'Like that,' she said, 'only louder.'

'You behaving?'

'Nope.'

'Good. Beds full yet?'

'Yes, all full. Look, do you actually want anything, or what? Only it's really cold standing here in just flippers and a snorkel and I've got Tony tied up in the bathroom waiting for me to start whipping him . . .'

'Bye-bye.'

'Cheerio.'

The sun went down in a golden blaze and the queue for the lavatory began to lengthen.

Rachel found Tony listening to Mog in the kitchen.

'. . . and they started this hamster farm where they bred hamsters which were put through mincers,' Mog was explaining, '. . . so that they could mash 'em up and make jam which they'd sell to Dutch people to use as fertiliser for their tulips. And every year, as the tulip bulbs were planted, all the growers would form a circle around the tulip beds and sing "When its spring again, We'll bring again, Tulips from hamster jam . . .".'

Rachel went and found Ben. 'Thanks for the prezzy.'

'Good, isn't it?' said Ben. 'I've got one in my squat.

Everything I own's got "Property of Benjamin Ronchetti" stamped on it – even the loo paper.'

Someone came staggering out of the upstairs lavatory clutching the loo-roll holder. 'It came off in my hand.'

The food table looked as though a bomb had hit it: worse – it looked like it had been savaged by sixty or so teenagers.

An entire pint of beer was spilled over the front room carpet and cigarette butts floated in half-empty glasses.

'We don't *need* meat in this day and age,' Lucy was telling Mog, whom for some reason she found fascinating. 'We can get all the protein we need from pulses, vegetables, fruit . . .'

'I'm allergic to fruit,' said Mog. 'It brings me out in a rash.'

'I've heard of that. It's got some long scientific name, hasn't it?'

'Windupeus terribulus . . .' said Mog, keeping an absolutely straight face.

'Yes. That's it. You poor thing. How are you with vegetables?'

Mog shook his head. 'Can't bear them. It's raw meat or nothing. My mum reckons it's 'cos I used to eat ants when I was a toddler . . .'

'Ants . . .?'

Mog nodded solemnly. 'And termites. My mum was frightened by an anteater while she was on the delivery table – that's what did it.'

Lucy thumped his arm. 'You're having me on.'

Chris was still hounding Annabel.

'Gissa dance . . .'

'Get stuffed, will you?'

'I only wanna dance. What's up with you? Why won't you dance with me?'

'I don't like you.'

'Why not? C'mon, why don't you like me? What's wrong with me?'

Annabel made a dive for the front room and got lost in the melee.

'Rachel,' Rebecca pulled her sister out of a ring of people. 'Here a minute.'

'What?'

'Present.' She pushed something into Rachel's hand.

'It's not for you,' she said. 'It's for you to give to Tony. You'll see.'

Rachel opened her palm. It was the size and shape of an egg, covered in scarlet glitter.

'What is it?'

'You'll see. Good luck.' Rebecca walked unsteadily along the hall and vanished into the dining room where Steven and a few others were playing a very disorganised game of poker.

The two halves of the egg broke apart with a half-turn. Inside was a plump red satin heart. It felt cool to her fingers — cool and solid — as though stuffed to the point of bursting. She enveloped it in her palm — her eyes skittering round to see whether anyone had noticed. The warmth of her hand was drawn into the shiny cushion. She could almost feel the blood pulsing through her wrist. After a few moments she pushed the egg-halves and the heart into her pocket and decided to search for Tony.

There were bodies everywhere and one or two people were beginning to drift off for last buses home.

'Polypin empty,' shouted someone from the kitchen.

Someone slipped on a dropped samosa and knocked the vegetable rack over. An impromptu game of bowls began on the swimming, mud-grimed kitchen floor — onions versus potatoes.

Chris sat on the garden steps.

'Why doesn't your sister like me?' he bawled at Cornell as he lurched past in search of lager.

'She doesn't like boys,' said Cornell, wavering in front of Chris. 'It's not you. She doesn't go out with boys any more. Not for a couple of years now. Didn't you know?'

'What? None at all?'

'None at all at all. She's moved on.'

'What's that mean?'

'She's moved on,' repeated Cornell, as though he thought that saying it twice would make it clearer. 'On and up.' Chris stared blankly at him. 'How old are you?' asked Cornell.

'Seventeen – nearly eighteen . . .'

'Not thirty-six? Well – there's your problem . . . you lack:' what should he say? 'You lack nineteen years for Annabel.'

'What?'

'Oh, forget it. I'm sure all will be revealed at some later stage . . .'

Tony was in the queue for the lavatory.

'Hello.'

'Hello.' Rachel jiggled the pendant and grinned. 'Shall I get us a drink?'

'Good.'

'I'll wait over there . . .' she pointed to the stairs leading up to the second landing.

Tony was about ten minutes. Rachel was sitting on the stairs with two cans of beer. 'There's not a lot left – hogs!' she said. Tony sat below her with his back to the wall, his head resting against her knees.

'I feel a bit tired,' he said. 'Or drunk,' he looked at her through his eyelashes. 'Or possibly both. Tired and drunk and driered and tunk. That's funny, the banisters are all moving about . . .'

'P'raps you shouldn't have any more for a while,' said Rachel who was feeling dreamy but quite sharp-witted, as though everything except herself was slightly out of focus.

'P'raps not.' She toyed with his hair, liking the weight of his head against her knees.

'Don't fall asleep,' she said.

'I'm not.' He looked up at her. He moved round to kneel on the stairs, his arms across her knees and his head resting on top. She stroked his face lightly with her fingertips.

'You're ever so beautiful . . .' he said. 'Have I ever told you that?'

'Not properly,' said Rachel. 'Not so I thought you really meant it.'

In the kitchen Mog and Lucy were sitting on the floor in the corner behind the fridge with their arms loosely around each other's shoulders.

'I'm thirty-two,' she was telling him, 'and I hate lentils . . .'

'Let me take you away from all this,' said Mog, his head slipping down on to her shoulder. 'Let me take you away to the kasbah . . .'

She stroked his hair with cold fingertips. 'They all say that,' she said, 'and it always turns into a back bedroom in Mitcham . . .'

'I think I love you . . .'

'No you don't . . .'

'No. I don't . . .'

Chris toppled backwards off the garden steps and lay in the grass staring up at the swimming sky. Mauve clouds on a purple field.

'You all right?' asked someone.

'Great,' said Chris.

'I'm off for a slash in the bushes . . .'

'Great . . .'

The doorbell rang. Someone had telephoned for a cab.

Rebecca staggered into the front room and turned the music down a bit. The leaping about had got less frenzied and some couples were actually dancing with their arms around each other.

'Lucy, I think we'd better go home now.'

Lucy looked blearily up. 'Hello, Daniel. This is Mog. Mog, this is Daniel.' Mog wiggled his fingers. Daniel pulled Lucy to her feet. 'Bye-bye, Mog, it's been lovely meeting you.'

'Likewise,' said Mog. 'We must do it again sometime.'

There was a lot of shouting from the dining room. The card game was getting a bit boisterous.

'What's "rabbit" mean?' asked Tony, his head in Rachel's lap.

'You still don't know?'

'Nope. Grandad said it must mean you want to breed with me . . . like rabbits . . .'

'Clever chap, your grandad.'

'Yes I know. He knows lots of things – but he's so old – I feel as if I ought to be spending all my time in there with him, pumping things out of him while there's still time – know what I mean?' He blinked stupidly. 'What did you say?'

'I didn't say anything,' stroking his hair.

'You did . . . about my grandad . . .'

'Clever. I said he was clever.'

'Clever . . .?'

'There's something I've got to tell you, Tony.'

Tony stared up at her with his mouth half-open; she sounded so deadly serious that he was half-afraid of what she might say.

Mog found Chris spreadeagled on the lawn in a pool of window-light.

'Get up, you clown. It's poster time.'

'I'd forgotten about it,' said Chris, scrambling up.

They dug out the photoposter.

'Got any Sellotape?' Mog asked Rebecca, who had joined the card game.

'Kitchen drawer – left hand. Why?'

'Surprise.'

Rachel took out the padded satin heart and handed it to him. They were alone on the stairs although she may not have cared anyway by then. She couldn't see anything but him.

'It's mine,' said Rachel. 'And I want you to have it.'

'Does it do anything?' asked Tony. He thought maybe it was a joke, the point of which he couldn't quite see.

'Oh . . . *Tony!*'

It slipped out of his fingers and fell into her lap. He retrieved it. The touch of his fingers against her shocked them both into silence.

With an awkward, gauche action, she took his hand and

kissed his knuckles, holding the backs of his fingers against her cheek — staring at him — trying to stare her feelings into him.

'Rachel . . .?' It was like a spring tightening in his chest.

'Yes?'

'Rachel! Ra-a-achel! Come out, come out, wherever you are!'

'That's Mog,' said Tony. 'What's he want?'

'Ra-a-a-chel!'

There was a lot of suppressed giggling in the front room. Chris was going round gathering people together. 'It'll be worth it,' he told them, 'just wait in the front room. It's a surprise.' Annabel and the older man were having a very intense conversation in a corner of the dining room floor. As Chris approached, they slid their arms obliviously around each other and kissed. Chris rocked back as if he'd hit an invisible wall. He stared at them for a second then went off to gather some more people. The card players ignored him.

'I'd better go down,' said Rachel.

'I'll come . . .'

'Come on then, let's find out what all the noise is.'

'Hang on,' said Chris at the foot of the stairs. 'Blindfold first.' Finally discovering the reason for Annabel's rejections made him spiteful. He wound a scarf round her eyes. She was smiling.

'What's going on?'

'You'll see . . .' said Chris, guiding her into the front room.

Mog suddenly looked unhappy. He glanced at Tony. 'Chris,' he said, 'I don't think this is such . . .' But it was too late. Chris positioned Rachel in front of the poster. She could sense the people around her and hear stifled giggling.

'What *is* it?' said Rachel.

'Surprise!' shouted Chris, pulling the blindfold away. There was a collective yell of laughter and a vicious burst of applause.

Rachel's smile died.

If she hadn't spent the evening at such a peak of joy then perhaps the poster would not have shattered her happiness so completely. If everything had not been so perfect . . .

Mog grabbed Tony's arm, trying to stop him entering the front room – but there was a nasty edge to the blare of laughter that made Tony shake him off and push through. Rachel was just standing there. Tony followed the line of her eyes to the poster. He made a move, but Rachel moved first, blundering out of the room with a low moan like a distressed animal.

She ran down the hall, through the kitchen and out into the garden. She tripped on the steps and fell – hurting herself. She stood swaying in the middle of the lawn, her eyes tightly shut, her mouth open in a scream that wouldn't come. The humiliation and pain and spite rose up in her like acid and she was violently sick.

Rebecca ran into the front room, drawn by the noise. She stared at the ugly poster. Her face went white. 'Ben!' she shouted. Her brother appeared, frowning. She pointed at the poster. The laughter of the party guests died away into an uneasy silence.

'Who did this?' asked Ben, blazing with a sudden anger.

'Him,' said Chris, pointing at Tony, too drunk to care about the consequences.

Tony didn't even see the punch coming. There was a sudden, blinding pain that filled his face and he felt his legs give way under him. He hurt as though he was being hit over and over again, but it might have been just that one great pain reverberating through his body. There was darkness and a bitter taste in his mouth and the impression of tumbling down an endless, rock-strewn hillside.

Chapter 13

Why were all the lights on? Tony stood at the gate, gathering himself. He wasn't sure how he'd got there – carried? driven? walked? The last half hour was a pain-filled blur and it was not until he stood staring up into all the lighted windows of his home that he came fully to his senses.

'Taxi . . .' he murmured. His mouth hurt. Mog had brought him home in a taxi. That was it.

But why were all the lights on? It was well past midnight – a long way past midnight. Everyone should have been in bed hours ago – but the hall light shone yellow through the glass of the front door, the front room window glowed red and, upstairs, grandfather's window burned a smoky blue.

He let himself in. He ached all over but the pain seemed concentrated particularly in a broad area from his left eye to his jawline. He walked quietly upstairs to the bathroom and washed the dried blood off his chin where a tooth had cut his lip. He was stonily sober but the pain made him feel unsteady, almost like a different, more horrible, sort of drunkenness.

'Tony?' His father's voice called up the stairs.

There were drops of blood on his shirt. He walked back down in a daze, expecting an eruption of anger.

'What have you done to yourself?' His father's voice was strangely quiet – subdued.

'I got hit . . .'

From the front room he heard his brother's voice: 'He never liked me, anyway . . .'

'What's going on?' asked Tony.

'It's your grandfather . . .'

Tony ran upstairs. His grandfather's bed was a confused muddle – empty. Apart from that there was nothing obviously wrong.

His father stood in the doorway. 'We found him on the floor.'

'Where is he?'

'He must have . . . he must have been . . .' his father's voice died away. 'It must have been instantaneous.'

'What must?'

'The ambulance men wouldn't take him – they said he'd been dead for three hours. We had to get his own doctor.'

Tony sat on the edge of the bed.

'Are you all right?'

'Yes. Well . . .' he made a motion, indicating the swollen and ruddied cheek.

'Come down,' his father held out his arm. 'Come on down to your mother . . .'

'No. Can't I stay?'

His father nodded. 'If you like. Do you want some coffee?'

'No. Yes. Yes, okay . . .'

Alone in the room Tony fell back on to the bed. He stared up at the ceiling. He began to laugh softly, a dry, broken sound. Near the light-fitting in the centre of the white expanse he could see a yellowy patch that he had missed. He hadn't even been able to do that properly – he couldn't even do a simple thing like painting a ceiling properly.

Rachel woke up to Rebecca's anxious face and a glass of orange juice.

'. . . We'd better clear up . . .' she said.

'We've done it, sweetheart — it's already been done.'

'What time is it?'

'Ten o'clock — just about.'

Rachel sat up. 'What happened? I'm not trying to be funny, I remember being sick all over the place . . .'

'You passed out,' said Rebecca, sitting on the bed. She ran the backs of her fingers over Rachel's forehead. 'Uck!' she said. 'All sweaty and horrid . . . why don't you have a nice bath?'

'Where's Tony? Did he stay?' She made a smoothing gesture of the duvet to one side of her — her face rueful.

'He got a taxi . . .' Rebecca screwed up her shoulders like someone trying to ease an inaccessible itch. 'There was some trouble.'

'I haven't got a headache or anything,' said Rachel, vaguely, '. . . I must have had a lot to drink.' She looked up. 'What sort of trouble?'

'It was Ben . . .'

'Oh, God! What did he do?' Ben was famous for trouble.

'There was a mix-up — Ben thought Tony was responsible for the picture — that nasty picture — and he . . . well . . . he hit him . . .'

'Why? Oh, God . . . bloody Ben! Was he all right? Was it bad?'

'It got a bit messy. He just about knocked Tony out flat — then that bloke Chris, and his mate, the little one, piled in on Ben and then Cornell steamed in as well . . .'

'. . . Christ . . .'

'We managed to get them apart and get it all calmed down. Mog . . . that's his name, isn't it? . . . Mog was really good. That Chris was so pissed he could hardly stand up, and he was ranting about Annabel. I think someone must have told him — or he'd seen something — with Joe — but Mog managed to get through to Ben that it wasn't anything to do with Tony at all. They just ended up kicking Chris out. Then we phoned for a taxi for Tony and Mog took him home. Ben's feeling incredibly bad about it. You know what he gets like. You'll have to forgive him . . .'

'What about Tony . . . Christ! . . .' she laughed, although it wasn't funny. 'I feel like I've lost a million pounds and found fivepence . . .'

'It's nothing that can't be mended,' said Rebecca. 'Come on, I'll run a bath for you. You can use some of those bath-pearls Mum got you . . . have a good soak . . . then you can phone Tony and . . .'

'And what?'

'I don't know. And carry on from where you left off . . .'

'Where did I leave off?'

'I'll run you a bath . . .'

'I'll phone him first.'

'Okay. But don't be ages or it'll get cold.'

Rebecca liked to be useful. She went into the bathroom, turned on the taps and dropped half a dozen silky bath-pearls into the swirling water. A rich scent rose up almost immediately. She checked that there were clean towels and spread the big white one over the warming rail. She went to Rachel's room and collected her dressing gown and slippers – knowing Rachel would forget them. She went back to the bathroom with them, and swished the steamy water about with her fingers. Had Rachel taken out her contact lenses? Probably not. More aching eyes . . .

Rachel stood at the doorway in her crumpled cotton nightgown. She looked completely bewildered.

'Now what?' said Rebecca gently.

'It's . . . Tony's grandfather died . . . during the night . . . I spoke to his mother – to Tony's mother, I mean – he had a heart attack. Tony and his father are out making arrangements or something . . .'

'Oh . . . that's sad . . .'

Rachel held her hand to her mouth, her stomach heaving.

'Are you going to be sick?'

'Yes . . .'

'Come on, let's get you to the loo . . .'

'. . . he was . . .' Rachel swallowed hard, '. . . he was the only one that understood what . . . rabbit . . . meant . . .'

Chapter 14

Rachel intended to telephone Tony that evening, but when it came to it she just couldn't bring herself to pick up the receiver. She knew how close he had been to his grandfather and somehow she felt that she would be intruding on private grief. She didn't know if she was close enough to Tony to share the experience with him.

'I don't know what to tell you . . .' said Rebecca. 'Mum'll be home soon. She'll know what to do.'

'I can't tell Mum . . .'

'Of course you can . . .'

'No. Don't.'

Their mother had come home in the middle of the afternoon but had been too preoccupied with fussing over Ben even to notice how depressed Rachel was. And Rachel was very good at keeping herself to herself in times of crisis. Rebecca was vowed to silence.

Ben stayed until Saturday and it was not really until that evening that their mother looked up, as it were, and noticed the absence of her younger daughter.

'She's in her room,' said Rebecca.

'Doing what?'

'Moping. Look, she told me not to say anything to you,

but, well . . .' and then the whole story came tumbling out.

'Sweetheart? Can I come in?'

'Yes.' Rachel was in her old armchair – a throw-out from the front room – curled into a ball, reading.

'What's that?' asked her mother. The window was open and a light breeze made the room airy. 'Look at that sunset.'

'Mm . . . I know.' Rachel held the book up. D. H. Lawrence: *Women in Love*.

'That won't cheer you up . . .' said her mother.

'I'm all right . . .'

Her mother knelt on her heels, her elbows on the arm of Rachel's chair. 'Look at the colours out there . . .'

Rachel looked.

'Why don't you phone him?'

Rachel stared down at the book – not seeing it. She could say 'Phone who?' but that would just be playing games; she could say 'I don't want to' but that would be so blatant a lie that it would have stuck in her throat.

'I don't know . . .' she murmured.

'Are you scared?'

'Yes . . .' Her mother put her arms round her.

'You silly goose . . .'

Rachel laughed sadly. 'Goose? Why goose?'

'Because.'

'That's daft.'

'It made you laugh, though.' Her mother squeezed her. 'It can't hurt to phone him. What's the worst that can happen?'

'I don't know . . . that's the whole problem . . .'

'Do you care for him very much?'

'Yes . . . very . . .'

'Phone him, then.'

'He could have phoned me. Why hasn't he phoned me?'

'There's a lot to do when someone dies. And, anyway, he might be afraid you . . . well, he might think you don't want to be involved. He might even think you haven't forgiven him about the photograph-thing.'

'You know about that?'

'Yes. You are dozy – you should have just laughed, you know, and taken no notice.'

'Yes . . . I know . . . it didn't seem very funny at the time – but I still wish I'd said, "Oh, how *interesting*, a photograph of me looking fat and horrible – how amusing" and just shrugged it off. But it's easy, with hindsight, to know what you should've done, isn't it? Easy to say – *that* was stupid!'

'Ring him.'

'I will.'

'Now.'

'No. In the morning. I'll be up to it in the morning.'

'Good girl.'

Rachel smiled bleakly and gazed out into the burning sky. 'It's okay, I suppose . . .' she said, resting her head against her mother's shoulder '. . . if you like sunsets . . .'

'That's typical of you,' said Tony, sitting on the edge of his grandad's bed. 'You get some sort of perverse delight in doing the most awkward . . . irritating . . . bloody-minded thing you can, and then just sit back with that fiendish grin on your chops and watch us all running about like blue-arsed flies . . . you can't even wait until I get . . . you didn't even wait until I could say goodbye. You know, I think that's what really pisses me off about all this more than anything else – more than having to sit in that rotten hospital for three hours – more than that ugly old bitch at the death place – more than all the "sincere condolences" at the undertakers – the fact that you didn't even wait so I could say goodbye. Not even a "Cheerio, Laddo". I just come home and you've buggered off – just like that – without a word.'

It had my name on it, Laddo. You can't say: wait a minute, I've got to have a word with my grandson. They're not very patient, once your number's up.

'Oh, shut up, you miserable old sod.' Tony punched the pillow and stood up. 'Now look at me, you've got me talking

117

to myself. I'm standing here talking to an empty bed. Listen to me.' He walked over to the window. Back to the bed. Over to the window again. 'The fact is,' he said, 'and you'll like this one – this'll really appeal to your warped sense of humour. The fact is . . .'

The fact was that Tony had not realised how important his grandfather had become. It had happened so slowly that Tony hadn't seen it happening at all.

'Go and ask your grandad . . .' when Mum was ironing or busy cooking.

'I don't know – ask the old fellow . . .' when Dad was under the car.

'Don't ask me!' from Martin. 'How should I know?'

'Grandad, I've been thinking . . . Grandad, what if . . . Grandad, I want some advice . . .'

'Tea first – then sympathy. That's the order of things. Tea first.'

But after the tea the sympathy was always on tap, a huge, flooding lifetime of sympathy and now . . . and now there was just a void.

'An artist cannot work in a void.'

'You've dumped me right out in the middle of nowhere, you sod!' said Tony. 'I need to know what to do about Rachel and you're not even here to tell me . . .'

You'll think of something, Laddo.

'Tell me what? Oh, bloody hell – I've got to stop this.'

Tony ran down the stairs. Sunday morning and no smell of rancid old hand-rolling tobacco. No one whining for a cup of tea. As he closed the front door behind himself Tony heard the telephone ringing.

Rachel held her sister's hand painfully tightly.

'It's ringing,' she said.

'They tend to once you've dialled . . .' said Rebecca.

'He's picked it up!' Someone spoke at the other end.

'I'm sorry? What did . . .' Rachel put her hand over the

receiver. 'It's his brother,' she hissed to Rebecca. 'He's calling him.' There was a loud noise as Martin threw the receiver on to the table.

'What was that?' asked Rebecca.

'I think he put the phone down . . .' Rachel nibbled her top lip nervously. 'I feel so stupid . . .' she said, letting go of Rebecca's hand and then grabbing it again. '. . . I can hear him yelling.'

'Kids have got no idea . . .' said Rebecca, '. . . the poor old man's not even properly cold yet . . .'

'Sshhh . . .'

To Martin the death of 'the poor old man' had been about as traumatic as a grazed knee. A lot of immediate pain and shouting, but a very rapid return to normality. On Wednesday Grandad had been there – on Thursday he wasn't. 'At least it's one less to argue over what we watch on telly . . .' 'Martin – that's a wicked thing to say.' 'Is it? Why?' And no amount of whys could persuade him into mourning.

'Do I have to go to the funeral?' 'Of course you do.' 'Oh, well – day off school, at least . . .'

'What if he won't talk to me?' asked Rachel.

'What if he will?' suggested Rebecca.

The phone at the other end was picked up. Martin told her that Tony wasn't in.

'Do you know where he is? . . . Do you know when he'll be back? . . . Has he been out long? . . . Hello? Has he been out long? . . . Will you tell him I rang? Tell him Rachel rang . . . Tell him . . .' There was a click. Rachel stared at the receiver. 'He's hung up.' She slowly put the receiver down. 'He wasn't in.'

'I gathered,' said Rebecca.

'Unless he told his brother . . .'

'Rachel!'

'I'm going round there.' She stood up, releasing her sister's hand.

Rebecca shook her hand and blew on it. 'Good,' she said.

'About time.'

Rachel ran up to her room. She wanted to wear something special — something that would dazzle him. Something that would bring out of him a look like the one on his face as she first walked down the stairs at the party.

'I can't think of anything,' she said, her heart hammering. 'I can't *think* of anything.'

She looked at herself in the mirror. Tee-shirt and jeans. She still looked a bit bulgy but she could hide that and there simply wasn't time to change. She had to get there as quickly as possible. It was like a race — every second was vital. She threw on a denim jacket and grabbed up her shoulder-bag. Without quite knowing why, she put the birthday present from her brother into the bag.

She was halfway down the stairs when she remembered the necklace. With a growl of annoyance she pelted back up and snatched it from the dressing table, cramming it into her pocket.

Her father was in the hall.

'Where are you haring off to?'

'Hunting rabbit,' said Rachel, running past.

The door shivered as she slammed it.

'No one takes a blind bit of notice of me in this household,' he said aloud. 'I might as well be the Speaker of the House of Commons . . .'

'What on earth was that?' Mother from the front room — up to her eyeballs in the *Observer*.

'Our lesser daughter has just gone out. Hunting rabbits, apparently, whatever that's supposed to mean . . .'

'About time too.'

'That's what I said,' said Rebecca, coming out of the kitchen.

'I wish I knew what was going on,' said her father. 'Will someone tell me what hunting rabbits means?'

Rebecca patted his cheek in passing. 'No,' she said, smiling. 'But keep your fingers crossed.'

Chapter 15

'Hello. Mrs Anderson? It is Mrs Anderson, isn't it? I'm sorry to bother you. Is Tony in, at all?'

'You're Rachel, aren't you?' Tony's mother had been in her father's room clearing out the wardrobe and putting things into black plastic bags for the Salvation Army.

'That's right.'

Mrs Anderson nodded. 'I've seen pictures of you . . . drawings, of Tony's . . .'

Tony's father came out of the kitchen with half a sandwich in his hand. 'What is it, pet? If it's Jehovah's Witnesses tell them . . .'

'It's Tony's friend from school. The one in all the drawings.'

'Oh.' He retreated back into the kitchen.

'He's gone out, dear. Was he expecting you?'

'No. I just thought he might be in.'

'They're just like you.'

'Sorry?'

'His drawings. They're just like you.' She smiled. 'We hope he'll go to college.'

Rachel couldn't think of any sensible reply to this.

'I'm sorry about . . . I was sorry about his grandfather . . .'

'At least it was quick.' As though this was supposed to be of some comfort. 'Would you like to come in and wait? He shouldn't be long.'

'No. No – thanks all the same – I don't think I will. Tell him I called. Will you tell him I called, please?'

Rachel stood forlornly on the street corner. *'At least it was quick.'* Someone you loved died and the best that could be said was 'at least it was quick'. Rachel shivered . . .

'What would you like for your birthday?'

'A surprise.'

'What sort of surprise?'

'A surprising surprise.'

Rachel remembered their evening in Nunhead Cemetery, Tony stretched out in the grass while she sketched him.

'It was my grandad first brought me here,' she remembered him saying. *'See this?'* A granite obelisk. *'Its a monument to some Scottish martyrs . . . something to do with Parliamentary Reform . . . there's one exactly the same in Glasgow . . .'*

Nunhead Cemetery.

If Tony was anywhere in the world then he would be at Nunhead Cemetery.

She found him lying in the grass in the same place as before. He was flat on his stomach with his head cradled in his arms, as though he was asleep. She stood in tree-shadow, watching him – wondering what he was thinking – and whether she dared to make a move towards him.

She circled soft-footed round him and sat quietly, cross-legged, at his head-end, about five yards distant. She wished she had brought a sketch pad – drawing him foreshortened like that would have been a useful exercise – to say the least. She found herself thinking that she would like to kiss him all over. Ronchetti! Behave yourself! she thought.

She pulled the necklace out of her pocket and clasped it round her neck. She looked down at it – stroking the stripy brown stone with the tip of her little finger. Actually wearing it made her more confident. She rested her hands in her lap and closed her eyes. Rebecca was into yoga. Deep breathing. That was a calming technique. Long ... slow ... deep breaths.

She opened her eyes and was prepared.

'Tony?'

His head moved slightly.

'To-ony?'

He rubbed his eyes against his forearms and looked up. His eyes widened but he didn't say a word.

Rachel saw immediately the livid purple bruise beneath his left eye.

She scrambled towards him as he sat up in the grass.

'Your poor face.' His lower lip was swollen and there was a small cut near the corner. She held his face between her hands and kissed him gently on his wounds. 'Bloody Ben!' she said, touching her forehead against his. 'I wish I'd known. I'd have kicked him all the way back to Leeds – the rotten swine.'

'I'm all right ...' He smiled. 'Ow.' He touched his lip. 'Hurts ...' he said.

'Only when you laugh ...'

'Something like that.'

'What about your eye? It looks horrible.'

'Thanks.'

'Did you put a raw steak on it?'

'No. A beefburger.'

'You didn't?'

'No. I didn't. I was dreaming about you.'

'When?'

'Just then. I was having a dream about you and when I looked up there you were. I couldn't believe my eyes at first. I thought I was seeing things.'

'But it was me. Solid me.'

Tony slid his hands around her waist inside her jacket.

'Try not to notice the squashy bits,' she said defensively.

'I've still got some to lose.'

He stroked the softness above the line of her jeans. 'Not for my benefit,' he said. 'I like you as you are.'

'Do you? Wouldn't you rather I was more sort of Clews-shaped?'

'Not especially. I couldn't . . . like you more than I do now whatever you did. Not unless there was two of me.'

'What was I doing – in your dream?'

'You'll laugh.'

'Tell me.'

'You were saving me from an 'orrible ravening monster.'

'Was I?' Rachel grinned.

'Yes. I was tied to a pole in the middle of a rocky valley. The 'orrible monster was going to eat me but you came galloping in on a white charger . . .'

'I bet that's dead Freudian. Did I have armour on?'

'I don't remember. I don't think so.'

'Did I have a lance or a sword?'

'Sword, I think. Why?'

'I'm just interested, go on.'

'That was it. Then I heard you calling my name and I woke up.'

'So we don't know if I actually saved you or not?'

'I'm sure you did.' He looked seriously at her. 'I've missed you.'

'I've missed you. I kept wanting to phone but feeling too wet to actually do it.'

'I wish you had. I felt so lonely.'

'You could have phoned me.'

'I didn't know if you still . . . well . . . you know . . . after that picture . . .'

'It's pathetic, isn't it? We're totally useless.'

'I'm used to asking Grandad . . . he doesn't . . . didn't always say what I wanted to hear, but . . . well . . . you know – I could at least trust him. But in the end I couldn't even trust him to stay alive a bit longer.'

'I'll stay alive . . .' she said, resting her arms across his shoulders. 'You can trust me to stay alive. Promise.'

She unclasped her shoulder-bag. 'I've got something for you,' she said. 'Close your eyes and hold out your hand.'

'Its not going to be something revolting, is it?'

'Don't be such a coward. Come on – do what you're told.'

Tony shut his eyes and stretched out a hand between them. Rachel took out the ink-pad and stamp.

She turned his hand over and pressed the stamp carefully on to the back.

'What's that?'

'Have a look.'

PROPERTY OF RACHEL RONCHETTI.

'There you are,' she said, 'that makes it official.'

He gazed, half-smiling, at the imprint, then looked up at her.

'Will you make love with me?'

She looked solemnly into his eyes. 'No,' she said softly.

'Oh . . .'

'I don't mean: no, never. I mean: no, not now.'

'But people always make love after someone's died – I've seen it in films . . .'

'This isn't films. Look, I've never made love with anyone before, and when we do it I want it to be just us – just you and me – I don't want you to start thinking about other things . . . about your grandad.'

'Will you come to the funeral with me?'

'When is it?'

'Tuesday.'

'I can't. I'll be at school, won't I? We'll see each other in the evening.'

Tony smiled crookedly. 'That'll help – knowing I'll be seeing you afterwards.'

'. . . and afterwards, and afterwards, and afterwards . . . for as long as you like.'

'I'd kiss you if my mouth didn't hurt.'

They knelt up, holding each other close.

'Rabbit . . .' said Tony.

'Rabbit back,' whispered Rachel, squeezing him tightly. 'Rabbit back and doubled.'

THE MOLE AND BEVERLEY MILLER

ALLAN FREWIN JONES

'It was Bev,' said Sophie, 'She's been knocked off her bike by a car.'

In a cool daze Michael allowed himself to be led into the kitchen. He sat at the table, staring out of the window at the wall of the house next door.

He relived their parting embrace; he always kept his eyes open so there could be no doubt that she was real. He had kissed too many phantoms.

Michael reflects on how his relationship with Beverley has grown while he waits and hopes that she will get better.

'One of the most believable, emotionally gripping and *real* teen novels I've read for a long time.'

Stephanie Nettell, *The Guardian*

THE COST OF GOING FREE

ALLAN FREWIN JONES

Tom Lane is handsome, different and daring. Everything in fact that Sally's mother and brother disapprove of. But why listen to them when the bright lights of the local fun fair and, more importantly, Tom beckon . . .?

'Intelligently written . . . earthy dialogue,'
British Book News

'I hope he proves full of books. Publishers are always saying so-and-so really understands how kids think and talk, but it's rarely true. This time it is!'
The Guardian